CU00920904

Living in the Subjunctive

Living in the Subjunctive

M J WALSH

Copyright © 2025 M J Walsh

The moral right of the author has been asserted.

Apart from any fair dealing for the purposes of research or private study,
or criticism or review, as permitted under the Copyright, Designs and Patents
Act 1988, this publication may only be reproduced, stored or transmitted, in
any form or by any means, with the prior permission in writing of the
publishers, or in the case of reprographic reproduction in accordance with
the terms of licences issued by the Copyright Licensing Agency. Enquiries
concerning reproduction outside those terms should be sent to the publishers.

This is a work of fiction. Names, characters, businesses, places, events
and incidents are either the products of the author's imagination
or used in a fictitious manner. Any resemblance to actual persons,
living or dead, or actual events is purely coincidental.

Troubador Publishing Ltd
Unit E2 Airfield Business Park,
Harrison Road, Market Harborough,
Leicestershire LE16 7UL
Tel: 0116 279 2299
Email: books@troubador.co.uk
Web: www.troubador.co.uk

From PABLO NERUDA SELECTED POEMS by Pablo Neruda. Copyright
© Estate of Pablo Neruda. Translation Copyright © Anthony Kerrigan, W.S.
Merwin, Alastair Reid and Nathaniel Tarn 1970. Poetry reproduced by
permission of The Random House Group Ltd.

ISBN 978 1 83628 189 4

British Library Cataloguing in Publication Data.
A catalogue record for this book is available from the British Library.

Printed and bound by CPI Group (UK) Ltd, Croydon, CR0 4YY
Typeset in 10.5pt Garamond Pro by Troubador Publishing Ltd, Leicester, UK

To those Chileans I knew who endured so much yet retained
such a generosity of spirit

To Maria for her assistance in finding readers

To Sara for reading an early draft and providing helpful
comments

To all my family who love me as I love them

Contents

Part I

Exodus

Chapter 1

I wake up to a noise coming from afar. It's the shriek of aeroplane engines accelerating, then slowing, before building up speed again and fading into the silent distance. More planes arrive to repeat the pattern. I stumble out of bed and pull open the heavy, velvet curtains to be blinded for a few moments by the brilliant light of the sun in a cloudless, blue sky.

Several miles away, I see fighter planes swoop down, one after the other, each dropping a single bomb, then soaring upwards in a wide arc over the centre of the city. A chill floods through my body. After a few minutes, I pull myself away and head for the stairs. With each step down, there is a growing dread, fuelled by more frequent explosions. Glancing at my watch, I wonder why it has stopped at seven o'clock in the morning of 11 September 1973.

I push open the door of the living room to be startled by the television turned up to high volume, which is odd at any time of day, most of all this early in the morning. In the armchair at the far end of the living room sits my father, leaning forward with his eyes fixed on the television screen. He is holding a half-eaten slice of toast in his left hand and a glass of sparkling wine in the other. Turning his head towards me, he smiles as he raises his glass in a celebratory manner and then takes a long sip before placing the glass down onto the coffee table with unnecessary force.

'I told you it would come to this. Not before time!'

'Can't you leave it, just for once?' my mother pleads in a weary voice. There is a duster hanging limply from her hand as she turns away from polishing the dining table. I am distracted by what is happening on the television screen in the corner of the room. There is something odd about the commentary. It's not the voice of a professional television reporter – it is much too stern in its tone and the staccato observations are delivered in an overexcited manner by someone who is ill at ease in the role. The commentator makes no attempt to conceal his support for the military attack on what is La Moneda, the presidential palace in the centre of Santiago de Chile, the capital of my country.

On the television screen, I see up close a continuous stream of planes swooping low over the palace at breakneck speed. Bombs explode in shocking and reverberating blasts, causing split-second flashes of orange fire, followed by plumes of black smoke drifting upwards into the cloudless sky. In an instant the screen changes from the pristine blue sky to street level, where rows of tanks line every side of the burning palace. Their gun turrets shudder at the firing of each shell as a steady stream of soldiers scamper through the grand palace entrance while others lie on the road outside, firing their machine guns and rifles at the now shattered windows of the palace frontage. I am struck by the contrast of the slow-rising smoke with the manic chaos in the surrounding streets, where the army is supplementing the air-force attacks with its own relentless assault. The only silence is that of my father and myself transfixed by the same television screen but seeing different realities.

Standing rigid and gripping the top of the sofa, nausea sets in. These are scenes of war – of civil war. I am not stirred to respond to my father's provocative cries of approval. Turning abruptly I leave the room preferring radio commentary rather than having to watch these scenes of imminent Armageddon. With each step up the staircase, hope fades that the outcome will be anything other than victory for the armed forces. After a few frantic minutes searching the airwaves on the radio, there is only one station to be found which is sympathetic to the Government. It reports again and again that a military coup was launched at dawn and calls on people to rise up and resist. Wasn't it only yesterday my friends and I talked of the rumours of a plot to overthrow the Government? We dismissed the suggestion as nothing more than another episode of the frequent scaremongering and destabilisation tactics from the right-wing elements of the media. How wrong we have been!

Surely I can't be a spectator to something I should be resisting. After a few moments, the idea comes to me to meet up with my friends without delay, given the country is likely to be under martial law before long, and that will mean imposed isolation. Despite the repeated warnings on the television and the many radio stations supporting the military – all demanding that everybody stays in their homes while threatening anybody who dares to venture onto the streets that they will be treated as an enemy of the State – I am determined to meet with my friends. To do nothing will only make things worse in the long run, so I dress in haste and rush downstairs. On approaching the front door, all of a sudden my mother is standing there blocking my route.

'Please don't go out. It's too dangerous.'

'Mum, I'm not going anywhere near our flat in the city centre where all the fighting is. Besides, Lucia is visiting her parents and is not due back home until the weekend. I'm going to meet with some of my friends in the café where they gather for breakfast most days. It's less than a ten-minute walk away.'

'Sergio, Sergio, he's going out,' my mother calls to my father. There is a wavering in her voice that delays me.

My father appears in the hall with no trace of the pleasure he was showing a short while ago.

'Don't be stupid! You know it's dangerous to go out there.'

'As if you care. Mum, please don't worry. I'll be back this evening – I promise.'

I slide past my mother as she stands forlorn with her head bowed, making no attempt to stop me. I pull open the door and rush outside hearing them both calling out to me – imploring me to come back. Bolting down the pathway onto the street, I slow down, then come to a standstill. This is a place that I know well yet there's something not right. Never before has there been such an eerie silence with not a single person to be seen on the street. Taking a few hesitant steps along the footpath, I catch glimpses of curtains twitching in the windows of several of the houses on both sides of the deserted street. I up my pace. Aren't those spies now picking up their phones to report me to the armed force? I pull my collar up and my cap down to make identification more difficult. I break into a run, desperate to get away from those invasive eyes.

After a prolonged period under surveillance, the café comes into view at the bottom of the hill. Rushing in, my eyes are drawn to my four friends sitting at a table in the back corner, by a window with the blinds pulled halfway down. They and the young people at the other tables are listening to the commentary on the coup from a radio turned up to high volume, which is perched on a shelf above the coffee machine. The only person in the café not showing any interest is the owner, whose usual gruff demeanour is reassuring amid the chilling violence in the city centre.

'Anybody for a drink?' I call over to my friends.

Only Julia asks for a black coffee. I order two black coffees and only when spilling them while walking back to the table do I notice that my hands are shaking.

'Have you been listening to what's going on?' Julia blurts out, while averting her gaze from me. I can see she has been crying.

'Yes! I've been watching it on the television and listening to the radio. It's both the army and the air force attacking the palace, and it's being reported that the navy and the police have also come out in support. What's the latest?'

'An announcement was broadcast a couple of minutes ago saying that the president is dead. Nothing has been heard from Government sources to counter this, so I fear it may be true,' adds Jose.

All of us sit with our heads bowed for a few moments until Sara breaks the silence.

'The worst has yet to come. They aren't going to stop with the removal of the Government. They'll come looking for people like us. We should contact Roberto. He'll have an idea of what we should do.'

'Best not to phone him – the military might be listening into phone conversations. There's little happening here in the suburbs, so it should be safe to go to Roberto's,' I suggest in a low voice.

There is agreement among us and we set off in Jose's car.

The streets are deserted as we drive out of Macul, heading away from the city centre. The military bombardment can still be heard, albeit ever fainter, as we head for what we see as a place of refuge. As the car turns into the street where Roberto lives, without warning we are faced with a military roadblock only yards ahead. Jose slams on the brakes and the car screeches to a halt inches from the military barrier. Soldiers rush to surround us, pointing rifles at the car and shouting at us to get out.

'It's contrary to military decree to be on the streets. Keep your hands up! Why are you here?' demands an officer.

Without warning, he slams his rifle butt into Jose's stomach. Jose slumps to his knees and starts to retch, then vomit.

'We are visiting a friend, who has been very sick for the last week. We are worried about him,' Sara responds, as she crouches to rub Jose's back.

'What's your friend's name? Where does he live?'

'Roberto Almagro and he lives at number 34 on the right down there,' I reply.

'He's not there, but we know where he is and we will take you there,' the officer replies, with a smirk spreading over his face.

'Thank you, but it's okay, officer. We'll go straight home and stay there until we are allowed to go out. Sorry for our mistake,' I blurt out.

'But I insist! Get into the van over there. All of you!' he shouts.

'Can't we just go home? We didn't mean to break any regulations,' Sara asks.

'Too late!'

We are bundled into the back of the van and it sets off at high-speed swerving around corners with tyres screeching, causing us to be thrown sideways and forwards. There are no windows in the rear of the van. Without warning, the vehicle takes a violent turn to the right and comes to a sudden halt, which sends us crashing against the solid panel behind the driver. The back doors are flung open, and we are faced with another group of soldiers with visors on, all of them with their rifles pointing at us.

'Get out!'

Soldiers push and pull us down a dimly lit tunnel and after passing through several corridors, we are thrust into a large rectangular room. The door is slammed shut behind us and then locked. The strip lighting on the low ceiling is intense after the darkness of the corridors. We look around, blinking in the bright light. The room is packed with people. There are windows with closed shutters beyond reach, high up towards the ceiling. The air smells stale. As my eyes get accustomed to the light, I see that there must be hundreds of people here, mainly men, but perhaps about a third women. Most of them squat on the floor while others lean against the dirty, grey walls of this place in which there is not a single item of furniture. I scan again and again from one end to the other and spot cameras high up in two corners of the room.

'I can't see Roberto. Can any of you?' I ask.

Each of my friends shakes their head so we search the floorspace for a place to sit. There is room on the far side, too near the stinking toilets, but the only place where all five of us can sit together. On reaching the space, Jose strikes up a conversation with a group of four men and two women to the right of us. One of them, a tall, skeletal man much older than we are, recounts in a matter-of-fact manner that every hour or so groups of people are taken from the room. Nobody has returned so far. He tells us that there have been regular additions of people being brought in and reckons that all the people are either political activists or trade unionists.

'How did they get you?' he asks.

'We were caught when going to see a friend, Roberto Almagro. He's about thirty years old, smallish, stocky, with a moustache and a neatly trimmed beard. You haven't seen him here, have you?' Sara asks.

'I can't think of anyone of that description, but I haven't been taking note of everyone who has come and gone from the room. He may have been here but taken out before we arrived.'

The man explains that nobody wants to say who they are, perhaps because they suspect that some in the room might be spies for the military. He advises us to be careful. At that moment, a group of six soldiers armed with sub-machine guns bursts into the room. They make their way towards our group but sweep past us as we get up. They order the man we were talking to and the five others in his group to walk ahead of them to the exit. All of a sudden, they are gone. We stand looking at each other for a few moments before we slump back down onto the floor. Nothing is said as we keep our gaze downwards.

'We shouldn't mention anything about Roberto other than our friendship at university. Let's deny being members of any political organisation. We just keep to the story that we met at university and became friends through our membership of the chess club. That's true after all! Agreed?' I ask.

My friends nod. The murmur of conversation in the room is only disturbed when armed soldiers enter and take away yet another group or deposit more frightened people into this packed space. Arrivals are happening at a growing frequency. We keep to ourselves with none of us keen to engage with anybody we do not know, except to give a brief greeting or to respond with a faint smile to any query. More time passes before an armed group of soldiers bursts in and then make their way towards us. We are ordered to stand up and walk ahead of them to the exit. There is a violent blow from the barrel of a rifle into the small of my back.

'Move, move,' I am ordered. I comply despite the sharp pain making it hard to walk.

Sara is just ahead of me and glances backwards for a moment and calls out to me, 'This is your fault.'

I am shocked by what she has said. How can that be true? Guilt envelops me but I can't figure out why. Through the doorway and down a dimly lit corridor, we are marched at a pace that none of us are used to walking. Without warning I am grabbed by my hair and hauled to the left – then pushed into a small room with a single, low-hanging light. There is a chair that is occupied on the far side of the table and a vacant one on this side, which I am thrown into. I am too afraid to take my eyes off the man sitting across the table. He is wearing an officer's uniform, with two soldiers standing on either side of him, their rifles aimed at me, held no more than six inches from my head. He looks like my father.

'Your name,' he demands.

I give it.

'And the names of your friends?'

I say nothing. The officer nods to the soldier on his right and without warning I am knocked off my chair by the force of a thudding blow to the side of my head from the butt of his rifle. Barely conscious and feeling sick, I am dragged up from the floor and pushed back onto the seat.

'Your friends' names?'

'Jose, Julia, Pepe and Sara.'

'Full names! Don't fuck me about!'

I give their full names and in that moment I have betrayed them.

'You and your friends are members of the Revolutionary Communist Party.'

'No, we're not. We aren't members of anything other than the university chess club.'

'You're lying.'

'I'm not. Check with the chess club. That's how we know each other. That's how we are friends.'

The officer leans back in his chair and takes a long slow drag of his cigarette as he continues to fix his eyes on me. I try hard to hold his stare. His face breaks into a smile. I breathe easier.

'If you are lying to me, you cannot imagine what will happen to you. Anything more you want to say?'

'Nothing! I'm telling you the truth.'

I come to on a cold, concrete floor, with a throbbing pain in my neck and up the right side of my head. Nothing is visible in this place where there is not even a faint glimmer of light, and I know I have my eyes wide open. I run my hand up the front to my shirt collar and feel a sticky wetness that leaves a metallic odour on my fingers. It's my blood. Despite summoning all my energy, I cannot sit up and I give up trying after several exhausting attempts that make me feel I am about to pass out. The thought of my friends being beaten makes me wail. Terrified by what might come next, I think of my wife, Lucia, and wonder if she has also been detained. No, surely that can't be as she is staying with her parents miles from the city. In the darkness, I hold onto the comforting image of the Andes mountains that are ever present on the city's horizon, but that image fades as I struggle to stay conscious on this cold and unforgiving floor.

The silence is broken by the harsh sound in the distance of steel-capped boots on concrete, growing more menacing as they get closer and closer. The door is flung open. Torches are aimed at my face. I am hauled up off the floor, only to collapse when left unsupported. I am pulled by my legs out of the pitch-dark room into a corridor and dragged along on my back. All I can see is the wooden ceiling which is now visible in the dim light of the corridor. The pain in my head throbs in the delirium of noise from the steel-capped bootsteps of the soldiers, only inches away from my head. All of a sudden I am in daylight, but it's too intense for me to hold my eyes open to see what awaits. After a few seconds adjusting to the light, I turn my head in a slow movement from one side to the other. I am in a yard. The grey stone walls on all sides are about twenty feet high from my position, lying on the ground. I am hauled up and thrust onto a chair. My hands are tied behind the back of the chair so tightly that it feels as if the rope has cut into my wrists. I catch a glimpse of four others standing to my right side, staring into the distance, two of whom are women. None of them I recognise. All of a sudden I am plunged into darkness again as a thick blindfold is tied tight at the back of my head. Terror takes hold.

'Aim!'

Rifles are cocked. I'm gulping in air… My body is taut… I cry out, 'No! No! No!'

There is a violent jolt.

I am lying in bed, heart pounding, breathing hard. Relief surges over me with the realisation that it was the nightmare – the one of the period after the coup when I am about to be executed. How many times in the last two years have I woken up in this state? My eyes are drawn to the window where I can see the night stretching out into infinity. There is a faint glow in the dark sky, which is studded with countless, tiny stars sparkling in the quiet of the night. My breathing settles into a slow, steady rhythm and after a short time I sink into drowsiness that is pulling me into irresistible sleep. I force myself to sit up and reach to my right to switch on the bedside lamp. With an explosion of light comes certainty that I am safe from a return to the nightmare.

I get up and step towards the window to gaze up at the starlit sky and it is then that I catch sight of the full yellow moon to the far right. Relief has now transformed into resigned weariness, knowing that the nightmare will return during some night in the future, as it has always done. After countless episodes of the nightmare, I have become less sure of what is real and what is dream, with several questions and doubts remaining unresolved. As nothing has been heard or seen of my friends since, surely they must be dead. Why did I survive when they didn't is a question that I can never rid myself of. I feel the chill of the night, so I the open the bedroom door and step down the dark stairwell to the kitchen to make myself a hot drink.

Halfway down the stairs, a memory from last year comes to mind. My former wife, Lucia, is telling me, at the point when she had completed the packing of her belongings and was walking towards the front door of our home that she was relieved not only to be leaving our relationship but to be released from my nightmare. There was both envy and an inescapable loneliness when she said that. By that stage, our marriage had disintegrated into nothing but arguments and resentments, which in all honesty had been fermenting since those first weeks after the flight from our country to begin a new life in exile. For some time, I have been convinced that breaking up from my wife was an inevitable outcome of what had come to be after the coup. The truth is I was never again engaged with our life together, since being held captive and tortured. After the flight from Chile and arrival in England, the memories of those times have stalked me. Bit by bit the nightmare and its destructive impact contributed to the ending of not only the marriage but has restricted my capability to make lasting friendships and withered relationships shortly after they got started.

There have been periods of as long as a month when I have been free of the nightmare, only for it to re-emerge. Sometimes with me being awoken before the finale, because my wife had shaken me when she began to hear my fear-ridden murmurings, which she knew would shortly become shrieks of terror. In the first six months of exile, it can't be denied that my wife tried

14

as best she could to turn things around for us, but every idea she came up with to banish the nightmare failed. I tried all her suggestions: medication that aided deep sleep, not eating for at least four hours before going to bed, giving up alcohol, even hypnosis. None of them brought a sustained solution, although there were periods of time after applying any one of those hoped-for remedies, when I would sleep without trauma. However, like some ever-evolving virus, the nightmare always adapted and returned with no less ferocity than before.

Her last suggestion was that I should find a counsellor who could help me with what she reckoned must be a psychosis, now firmly embedded within me. By that stage, I had stopped listening to her and dismissed her view out of hand, to some extent because I wanted to do nothing that would prevent her leaving, such was my longing for relief from the wear of a broken relationship that was coming to an irrevocable end. I had dismissed her last idea because I could not face talking to anyone about my secrets. Yet, I have never given up on the possibility, albeit improbable, of being released from the nightmare. However, I have never been able to envisage how such relief could ever be brought about by efforts of mine. Despite the loss I still feel from time to time, I could never accuse her of lack of effort in trying to save our relationship.

So here I am, as so many times before, sitting at the kitchen table at around five o'clock in the morning, clutching a hot drink with both hands to extract the warmth from it, while trying to come up with some way that I have never thought of before of bringing closure to these exhausting episodes. As on all previous occasions, I reach the conclusion that everything has been tried. My attention drifts to my more recent friends, my fellow exiles from our distant homeland. The community of Chilean refugees has been my primary refuge. Through my involvement in the support of refugees here in England, undertaken to assuage my unresolved guilt, I have come to realise that I lack perspective when comparing my situation with those of the many others who have struggled to make their way through their hardship and grief. Indeed one or two of them have not made it through at all, so I can't have suffered as much as they did.

So much is unknown about our experiences, concealed from each other to some degree, but much more so from those whose lives have never been blighted by the torture and the ghosts of those we had to leave behind. All that loneliness, those hard, sometimes hopeless times, but more recently the welcome achievements in building a different life from the ruins of exile. How can people I meet here in England know what it is like to flee thousands of miles from one's homeland, to arrive in a place that is alien to what they have always known? On the other hand, I and most other refugees I know have enjoyed levels of kindness from many people here that we will never forget. What is seldom reported is the breathtaking generosity of those local people who help refugees through their first months of exile, and often much longer.

What was it that a couple of my compatriots often bemoaned? Yes, I remember it now. It was a complaint about how so many of the most interesting, human stories remain forever untold. That's why they encourage me to write and publish stories of exile, contending that not only would I be revealing those hidden stories to those who had no appreciation of being dislocated from their past, but that such a creative endeavour on my part could be a way of at least alleviating, if not resolving, what they referred to as 'my sadness'. They were not advocating more of the type of writing that I have always done, which consists of academic papers and articles in journals and newspapers on social and political matters impacting on Chilean refugees. Nor were they suggesting that I return to writing poetry as I had done in my youth.

What they were exhorting me to do was to write an authentic account of lives locked in exile, but written as fiction, either in the form of a novel or a set of short stories. As they put it to me – I could convey what is true by creating something that is not real. Their reasoning was that documentary accounts of what it is to live in exile restrict the exploration of the thoughts, feelings and secrets of those who manage to survive and even thrive, and also of those who never make it through to a better life. They argued that an authentic fictional story would get the reader nearer to the lived reality than a non-fiction account could ever do. As for the reliability of a person's memory in any non-fiction account, there were too many distortions and gaps which called into question whether one's memory can ever provide a full and true account of the lived reality.

On so many occasions they pushed me to take on this project, but my response has always been to resist, considering such writing to be beyond me. After all, I have never written fiction other than poetry, not even short stories, let alone a novel. And besides, my longstanding view has been that were I to attempt it, the insurmountable obstacles would be to produce coherent and authentic storylines and a failure to complete the book, due to my limited powers of endurance and sometimes feeble imagination. But now, sitting in the darkness with the break of dawn imminent, the idea of writing a story presents an appeal that has never been there for me before.

Perhaps it's because I have run out of any other idea of how to escape from an existence blighted by the nightmare and all within it that remains unresolved. Maybe I could manage to create something worthwhile, revealing stories worth telling which might also alleviate or even free me from my troubles. Yet surely such a book can never be completed until exile is over and justice delivered for my friends and the thousands of others.

Despite what looks like an impossible undertaking, I will embark on such a story. It may never be completed but that is not a good enough reason for not attempting it. With darkness melting into twilight and the dawn about to break, I start writing and begin to sketch out the first storyline. It is my last chance of being relieved from a past haunted by questions and doubts, a present with no shortage of insecurities, and a future never without uncertainty.

Chapter 2

There were few items of furniture in the dimly lit room: an ink-stained writing desk, an unvarnished wooden chair, a single bed with a mattress that sagged in the middle and a well-worn chest of drawers with a couple of handles missing. The walls looked as if they had not been painted for a generation. There was no carpet on the floor and the dirt-ingrained floorboards had long lost any trace of the warmth and scent of new pinewood. A large oval-shaped mirror with an uneven crack across the bottom half was hung above the wash basin in the corner, adjacent to a small window through which a shaft of daylight broke in to ease the pervading gloom. Carmen sat on the edge of the chair staring downwards. She was rubbing her index fingers and thumbs together and leaning forwards a few degrees as she rocked herself backwards and forward in a slow but unsteady rhythm.

She kept the door of her room locked from the inside in the refugee centre in Geneva. It was Sunday and she was immersed in thoughts of her homeland, catching onto images in her head of what she would have been doing on a Sunday, all those years ago before she had left the family home to start university in Santiago, about 350 miles from the town that she had been brought up in. The trace of a smile evaporated as her thoughts turned to the last year. Had it been only a year ago since she had fled Chile, accompanied by her boyfriend, Javi?

She got up and started to pace from one side of the room to the other. She had gone back in her mind to her flight from Chile. After the coup, she and her boyfriend had fled south to that region of Chile where turquoise-coloured lakes are surrounded by dense pine forests on the lower slopes of towering, snow-capped volcanoes. As they walked along a countryside road heading for the border with Argentina, there was an armoured car parked up ahead. Her stomach turned and nausea set in. In an instant, Carmen and her boyfriend turned off the road and rushed into the woods. After a few minutes of running at full pelt they were gasping for breath so stopped to rest for a brief period. Nobody had followed them.

They knew then that they had to keep off-road and make their way through the mountainous terrain of the Andes to get to Argentina. With the aid of maps that Javi had packed, they arrived in a country they assumed to be a safe haven, with the advantage of it bordering their homeland. And it was for the first few months, until one dark evening in the city of Córdoba on their way home from a political meeting opposing the Chilean coup. All of a sudden there were four armed men in front of them, wearing balaclavas. They were bundled into a black van at gunpoint. She could remember little after that and didn't want to try.

After being held in captivity in Argentina for almost a year, she was awoken on yet another of those countless, bleak mornings to be told, without any explanation, that she was to be released and deported to the United Nations Refugee Agency in Geneva, Switzerland. During that unbroken period of solitary confinement, she had not seen or spoken to her boyfriend, although on a few occasions she had caught sight of him from behind the bars of her unglazed cell window, when he was allowed a brief period of exercise in a small yard on the periphery of the building. Those out-of-reach sightings were as close as she had been to him until they were both released and driven together in a car on the long journey to Buenos Aires airport, where their handcuffs were removed, before being escorted to the boarding steps of a plane.

The flight from Argentina to Switzerland was like a dream for Carmen, throughout which she heard Javi talking and asking her a stream of questions to which she could only manage a single-word or short-phrase response. She flinched when he kissed and embraced just after they were released from handcuffs by the armed guard at the airport. An overwhelming exhaustion came over her a brief time after take-off and for the rest of the flight she drifted in and out of sleep, until awoken by Javi to be told they had just landed in Geneva. The process of disembarking, being met by UN refugee officials and then driven to the refugee centre near to the airport, was a blur. Despite being told by Javi that she was free, she had remained silent.

For a brief moment, the frown vanished from her face when told on arrival in the refugee centre that only single rooms were available, with men and women segregated into separate blocks, but with shared facilities provided for bathing, eating and recreation. On that first evening in Geneva, she wrote a letter of no more than a short paragraph to her mother in Chile telling her she was now safe in Switzerland, assuring her that she was in a good state of mind and physical health, and promising that she would write to her in more detail when she was happily settled somewhere more permanent. During every night that followed her arrival in Switzerland, she woke up in terror that she was still incarcerated in Argentina.

Most days in Geneva were spent trapped between the past year of which she could recall nothing other than unending misery, and a future that was full of uncertainty. The staff at the refugee centre formed the view that Carmen was traumatised and offered counselling, but she declined and assured them that she was better with each day and that they should have no worries about her.

Never having had access to a mirror during that long captivity in Argentina, she found herself spending a great deal of time in the refugee centre gazing into the cracked mirror in the corner of her room, as if getting reacquainted with herself. During those months in solitary confinement in Argentina, she had become convinced that, as with her mental state, her physical appearance must have changed so much that she would be unrecognisable. What she saw in the mirror provided reassurance that she had not mutated as she had feared, although on occasions she was compelled to look away and then quickly turn her eyes back, to check that the image was still there, unchanged.

What she was staring at for prolonged periods was a young woman who looked no more than her twenty-two years, with cropped, jet-black hair, brown almond eyes sunken by her high cheek bones and fulsome lips. All her features were locked within an expression of detached gloom. She despised her short hair as it was a stark reminder of captivity, so it would now be grown long, as it had been for as far back as she could ever remember… until that day in captivity when she had been tied to a chair. She had screamed in terror while two men cut her hair back to her scalp.

Since she had been accommodated in the refugee centre, Carmen was obsessed with minimising the amount of time spent in the company of others, especially Javi, with whom she was no less awkward than she had been on that long car journey to Buenos Aires airport, in those first moments of release from captivity. That awkwardness had now transformed into suspicion and on some occasions, fear, due to his constant attempts to be intimate with her. From the first day in the refugee centre, she spent most of the time alone in her room except for lunch, her single meal of the day when she ate as much as she could in an attempt to get through to lunch the next day, without having to leave her room for any more food or drink. She worked hard at keeping to a minimum the use of the bathroom that she shared with two other women refugees.

Although she did not raise an objection to Javi referring to her as his 'girlfriend' on the occasions when they ate together in the dining room in the company of others, there was not a single instance since they were released from captivity when there was not an onset of panic at any attempt at physical intimacy. Javi often walked back with her to her room after a meal, but she always refused to allow him entry. Each of his attempts at kissing and touching were met with firm resistance from her, and his persistence caused Carmen to then alter the times she went to eat each day.

Javi had shown no signs of trauma from his stay in prison and did not stop trying to be intimate with her. On the occasion when he took a firm hold of her head, forced a kiss on her lips while thrusting his hand up inside her top, Carmen had screamed at him. It was only then that he stopped trying. He accepted that the reason for her trauma was because she had been kept in solitary confinement for so long. That had been stated by Carmen herself as the cause. Javi did not respond to her promise that things would improve, although she advised him she had no idea when. He had already started to doubt that anything would ever change for the better.

While accommodated in the UN refugee centre, they were told that it was unlikely that they would have to wait long before resettlement was offered by one of several European countries that were accepting Chilean refugees. Eight weeks after their

23

arrival in Geneva, they each got an offer of resettlement in England. The destination offered was not down to chance, as it was for most of the other refugees, who were grateful to accept any country that made an offer. Javi had been brought up to speak English and Carmen had studied it at university in Chile, so being confident in the language, they had each asked for resettlement solely in the United Kingdom. The offer of resettlement in England was met with silence by Carmen who tried hard to remember why she had not pursued options of other countries. Javi smiled when told of resettlement in England.

Soon after take-off on the flight from Geneva to London, Carmen began to shake at the thought of what may lie ahead in a foreign country to which she no longer wanted to go. After all, she had nothing more than a basic knowledge of England, gained from her university studies. She became hot and flushed, gripped by a desperate longing for escape, rather than being trapped on this plane heading to a place that she was convinced would result in nothing but more terrible ordeals. She couldn't rid herself of the belief that on this journey she would die and that she would never see her family again. Gazing out of the window of the plane to the snow-covered Alps, some of which were higher than the plane for the quarter of an hour of climbing after take-off, a full-blown panic took hold.

She struggled for breath while unable to stop tears trickling down her cheeks to her chin, before dripping on to her light blue blouse. Her emotions being so exposed alarmed her but there was a little relief when she glanced at Javi and saw that he was so engrossed in reading an English newspaper that he remained unaware of the state she was in. Making herself breathe in and out in a long slow rhythm, the panic began to ease.

In less than a couple of hours since leaving Geneva,

Carmen was walking down the steps of the plane at Heathrow airport, concentrating on rhythmic breathing, and not noticing how chilly it was for early summer in England. They arrived at Passport Control where she had to stand for several minutes, awaiting a response after presenting her papers provided by the UN Refugee Agency. Something was said to her by the Border staff but she did not understand. It was repeated but she still could not make out what was being said. When two staff appeared and led her away, she had a flashback to captivity where she was at the mercy of brutal guards. She collapsed. She was helped up and then led away to a small room nearby.

Twenty minutes later, Carmen passed through Immigration Control. When Javi told her he had been allowed through Border Control without any questions, she swore at him which prompted other passengers to turn around to look at them. She trailed a few steps behind him all the way to the Arrivals exit, where they had been told they would be met by a woman whose name was written in the printed instructions that they had been given before leaving Geneva. Just to the right of the barrier in the Arrivals Hall a tall, slim woman dressed in jeans and an open-necked top stood smiling, holding a small white placard above her head with their names written on it.

'Jane Osbourne?' Javi called out.

'Carmen and Javi?'

'Yes, that's us! We are very grateful to you,' replied Javi as he extended his hand, while Carmen stood at his side, trying to smile and giving a nod of her head.

'Welcome! Your English is good,' Jane said as she gave each of them an awkward hug and a kiss on both cheeks.

As they made their way out of the terminal building, Jane explained that she would be driving them to a city called Bristol. There they would be accommodated in student halls of residence at the university, as they were vacant during the university summer break, but she promised that permanent accommodation would be found for them before the students' return in late September. She explained that as the university accommodation comprised only single rooms and given that she understood them to be a couple, she and her husband would be willing to accommodate them in their home where they had a spare bedroom with a double bed, if that was what they preferred.

'We are happy with single rooms, aren't we?' Carmen replied without hesitation, turning to Javi with an expression on her face demanding agreement from him. After a brief pause, he nodded his head. On the walk to the car park, Jane explained that it would take well over two hours to get to their accommodation in Bristol and then gave them a brief outline of who she was and of the city. She worked as a psychology lecturer at the university and was meeting them because she, together with some other university colleagues, had set up a support group for Chilean refugees. The group would provide them with assistance on everything from clothing, to accessing health services, claiming Social Security benefits, through to finding employment or training opportunities.

She acknowledged that they would not be needing English-language tuition as other refugees did and told them of a range of training and employment opportunities on offer to enable them to become self-sufficient, although it may take some time before that stage was reached. Each of them would have an assigned 'support worker' from the group to provide personal advice and assistance on any matter of concern. Jane would be Carmen's support worker and a colleague called Rachel would be Javi's.

'You will meet other refugees from Chile, most of whom have been in England for several weeks or months. Some of them are now in work and living independently,' added Jane.

On hearing this, Carmen began to sob, gasping for breath.

'Thank you. Such kindness…' was all she could manage to say.

'Carmen, I can hardly imagine what you have been through. Do you want a coffee before we start the drive?' Jane asks.

Carmen was unable to say anything in response. Something was different. What she was hearing was the possibility of being safe and secure for the first time in what seemed an eternity.

'Don't worry, Jane, Carmen is still recovering from everything that has happened. I think it's best to continue on the journey,' said Javi.

As she sat motionless in the back seat of car, Javi placed his arm round her shoulders. Although she did not respond to his touch, she did not flinch from it. Carmen was breathing in a steady rhythm. Javi removed his arm from around her shoulders and both of them sat in silence, gazing out to this new world. Carmen's attention was drawn to the view from the car window on her left. She could not divert her eyes from the rich and verdant countryside even after it became a blur when the car was being driven at speed. The rolling fields, hedges and occasional woodland made her think of spring. How different this was from the scrubland terrain of Chile that she had known as a child and a young adult.

Next to her in the back of the car, Javi continued staring ahead through the windscreen to the traffic on the motorway. He was thinking of Carmen. He could not fathom why she had become so distant, doubting that she would ever want to be with him again. Hadn't he been nothing but kind to her? Why had all his efforts resulted in a growing distance between them? All the excitement he'd felt on the plane from Argentina and the expectation that he had when it was confirmed that England was to be their destination, now evaporated. He would be trapped in a foreign land that could only ever be a staging post for a return to the life in Chile he longed for.

In the driver's seat, Jane could not stop returning to those images of how distressed Carmen had been at the airport. At first she had not attached a great deal of significance to it given that she was a newly arriving refugee, but the degree of upset was not what she had seen in other refugees she had picked up on previous occasions. What Carmen must have gone through! She could not settle on what that might have been, reaching only a vague conclusion that that whatever it was, it must have been horrendous. Her focus wandered onto how she should try to help Carmen talk about her traumas. She settled on the view that the matter would best be left until some point in the future when Carmen was feeling stronger and had built up confidence in herself and in her new surroundings.

The drive from the outskirts of Bristol, through the city centre and then to the halls of residence dominated the attention of both Carmen and Javi. How different was the streetscape from their homeland. Nothing was familiar and the only aspect that chimed with the country they had known all their lives was the traffic congestion in the city centre. By the time the car pulled into a tree-lined driveway in the university area of the city, the impact of the stark difference make Javi feel he was on the wrong side of the world, while in Carmen's mind, it suggested a possibility of a new start.

They remained seated in the parked car until Jane invited them to get out. Following a little behind her to the door of the halls of residence, each of them carried a small canvas bag, containing their sole possessions, amounting to nothing more than a single change of clothes and a few toiletries that had been given them in the refugee centre in Geneva. On entering the building, they were greeted by an assembled group of people, including Rachel, who was to be Javi's support worker. After brief introductions, Jane wasted little time in taking Carmen off to her room, as she was concerned that any more protracted greeting may tip Carmen into yet another breakdown.

Carmen looked around on entering the room, which had its own toilet and shower, and appeared to have been newly furnished. It was spacious enough to have an area in the corner with a small sofa and armchair arranged around a coffee table, as well as a kitchen area with a cooker and a fridge. She started to smile as Jane showed her around, which prompted Jane to suggest that she take her around the entire halls of residence. While they strolled around all the facilities, Jane told her of an event that evening with food and drink provided, which had been organised to welcome her and Javi. Carmen stopped in her tracks.

'I'm not very hungry. After the journey from Switzerland I feel very tired. Do I have to go?'

'You don't have to stay for the whole thing but there will be other refugees who will be keen to meet you. Sometimes I can find meeting new people a bit daunting. If you like, I could come to collect you from your room and we can go together,' Jane suggested.

'Thank you. I'd be grateful if you would. It's been a long time since I have been in a group, I don't have to dress up, do I?'

'No, of course not.'

'Just as well, as I have nothing that is smart.'

'You look good how you are, Carmen. We have a wide range of women's clothes in our store that will fit you and there is funding available to buy personal items and toiletries. We could go together to the clothes store and also do some shopping in town for other essentials. Is that something you'd like to do tomorrow?'

'Yes, perhaps. I can't remember when I last made plans for tomorrow. Will the event this evening last long?'

Chapter 3

Of the people who turned up, most were Chileans who had been resettled in the city over the past year. After the introductions and welcome speech, Carmen stood alone looking down at the floor as other Chileans approached and started to talk to her in her native language of Castellano. Javi joined them, which made her wonder briefly why being alone in his presence caused feelings of anxiety, yet not when she was with him in a group. In conversation with others, Javi was no longer referring to Carmen as his girlfriend, but as his 'friend' with whom he had fled Chile, only to be separated for the best part of a year when in captivity. Carmen could think of nothing to say to anyone.

While Carmen avoided talking of her experiences, she listened with interest to accounts of how other refugees had come through the early weeks and months in exile, and how they were going about establishing an independent life for themselves, with some of them already in work. There were a number of people in the group, but she found herself taking interest in a woman called Isabel who said she came from the city of Temuco in southern Chile, which was the city with the largest population of Chile's main Indigenous community, the Mapuche. She thought that Isabel was maybe part Mapuche, but then was not sure of that.

Isabel had been in Bristol for five months and was now

living with her Chilean partner, Pablo, in a rented flat in the city. She had recently completed a two-month training course on welfare rights and was about to start voluntary work in an advice centre in the city. Beyond that, she had decided to enrol on a social-work qualification course starting in September, as she wanted to return to what she had done in Chile. Her partner, Pablo, had already started work as a nursing assistant in the local psychiatric hospital. What struck Carmen was Isabel's quiet and assured manner and the degree of interest and empathy she had for local people in a country where she had arrived not that long ago.

In the group conversations, everyone was keen to tell their story and to make acquaintance, but Carmen remained silent and positioned herself on the fringe of the group. Isabel wandered up to her and suggested that they sit on their own by the window.

'I remember my first days here. I felt overwhelmed having come from such a different time and place, where I lived without thinking. How is it for you, Carmen? It must be doubly hard given that prolonged period you spent in captivity in Argentina,' Isabel suggested.

Carmen gazed at the floor, trying hard to think of something to say in response. She was unable to and managed only to shrug her shoulders and try to smile, which amounted to no more than a fleeting change of expression.

'Sorry, Carmen. I appreciate that some of us have had a much more horrendous time than others. I was one of the more fortunate from what I have heard since being here. If I can help… if you do feel like talking with someone, I'm more than happy to listen,' Isabel said.

'I'm sorry but I can't talk about it. I know I should, but I just can't. Perhaps soon. What about you? What has been the worst thing since you arrived in Bristol?'

Carmen explained that although she had Pablo, there were frequent occasions when she desperately missed her family and friends left behind in Chile, her mother in particular. That had been the worst thing, but things had got better now that she could send and receive letters from her mother. When she lived in Santiago, they used to write to each other a couple of times a week, but contact was ended by the coup. None of the family knew who was alive or dead until they eventually managed to re-establish contact. Every week now, she would write to her mother and she always responded the following week.

'Are you in touch with your family and friends, Carmen?'

'I wrote to my mother for the first time since leaving Chile when I was in Geneva. Now that I am to be settled here in England, I will be in more regular contact with her and also with my brother. It's my immediate family I miss too, but nothing else really. All of the past now feels contaminated. It's not somewhere I want to return to.'

'The worst things in this life lose their impact over time. Trauma can change how we feel. I hope everything works out well for you. Being able to trust others again has been an important turnaround for both Pablo and me.'

Carmen smiled and thanked her. She nodded when Isabel suggested it would be good to meet up again sometime soon.

Javi had spent most of the evening talking with other Chilean men about the political situation in Chile, both as it had been leading up to the coup and what they understood had happened in the country since. Four of the Chileans he met that evening were members of the same political party he was in and although he had not known them in Chile, they discovered that they knew some party members in common. The prevailing view was that there was no imminent chance of the military standing down. Indeed, they were consolidating their hold on the country and showed every intention of ruling for the long term.

'We have to face up to living in exile for a very long time. What's your view, Javi?' asked Manuel, who had introduced himself as Secretary of the Forum for Chilean Refugees in England.

'I am not long out of captivity so I am not as well informed as you are, but I hope you are wrong about that. The thought of living for years on the other side of the world from my homeland is hard to bear. I am a Chilean and that's where I belong,' replied Javi.

'Were you held in detention in Chile?'

'No, I would have been picked up after the coup, but my then girlfriend and I managed to get over into Argentina where things were fine until we were kidnapped one night by some ultra-right activists and held captive for the best part of a year. I am not sure why they released us.'

'How bad was it?'

'Bad enough, but nowhere near as bad as it was for some, from what I have heard since getting to Switzerland.'

'A group of us meet up every week and you'd be very welcome. Speaking our language and discussing Chile makes us feel we are keeping our identity and beliefs alive. We have also set up a five-a-side football team. Come along if you like. We always go for a few beers afterwards.'

'I'd love to. Thank you.'

Only towards the end of the evening did Javi and Carmen find themselves sitting together.

'I've enjoyed this. Talking to fellow Chileans made me feel connected to where I belong. How about you?' Javi asked.

'At the start, I was anxious, but less so than I feared I would be. It will take a while before I get back to how I was. I met someone tonight who I think will help me with that.'

'I'd like to help you if you'd just let me. Why are so you distant from me now? It feels like I have done you some wrong, which I haven't, have I?'

'I know you mean well and that me being like this must be difficult for you, but I need time and space to come to terms with everything that has happened.'

'It's difficult for me too, Carmen. Can't we spend some time together, just us, like we used to?'

'Well, yes, but not right away. I can't just revert to how things were before being held in captivity.'

'How about we meet up for coffee on a regular basis perhaps? Tomorrow evening?'

Carmen did not want to embark on anything as soon as that but was worried that Javi would be upset if she did not agree.

'Okay. Where were you thinking?'

'How about the small common room, around seven tomorrow evening?'

The next day when Jane came to pick up Carmen as arranged, she raised the need to start the process of getting access to welfare benefits and health services, exploring training and employment opportunities, and beginning the process for moving to more permanent accommodation. She was unclear how Carmen wanted to proceed with those matters and asked whether she wanted to have a joint plan for her and Javi, explaining that such a plan could be developed with the involvement of herself and Javi's support worker, Rachel.

'He's not my boyfriend,' replied Carmen.

'Oh, sorry, Carmen! I must have got that wrong?'

'Well, he was when we fled Chile, but that was a long time ago.'

'From what Rachel told me, Javi still refers to you as his girlfriend.'

Carmen did not respond.

'I'm sorry, Carmen. I'll go with whatever you decide is best for you. You've been through a terrible time. If you want, I can arrange personal counselling to help you. We have done that for others who needed one-to-one help after the trauma they went through.'

'Where would I get this counselling? Would I have to go into hospital?'

'No, it doesn't involve going to hospital. I am a trained counsellor so I could provide it, or you could be referred to someone else who is qualified. Whatever you feel most comfortable with.'

'I'm not sure. I am not saying no, it's just that I need to think about it.'

'Those who went for counselling found it a great help. I'd be happy to arrange for you to talk to some of them. Just let me know if you want to do that.'

'I don't think I need to talk to anybody who has done it, but I promise to think about it.'

'Of course.'

'One other thing, Jane. Can our discussions remain between us? Javi has his own worker to help him and I'd prefer that you don't share anything about me with Rachel, who could then share it with Javi. I'd just feel better with that arrangement.'

'Certainly. I promise to keep everything confidential. Between us alone.'

'Thank you.'

'Shall we get going on the trip for those clothes and toiletries you need?'

'Yes, please. I can't remember when I last went shopping for clothes.'

Carmen now had several sets of clothes after existing so long with not much more than what she was wearing. In various combinations, she tried on her newly acquired clothes and while viewing herself in the mirror, all of a sudden she was taken aback at seeing herself smile for the first time since she could remember. Her thoughts then turned to choosing what to wear for her meeting with Javi that evening. A dark blue, pleated skirt and a cream cotton top with no collar was her preference, which she thought contrasted well with her jet-black hair that had now grown to the point where it was brushing her shoulders. Besides the clothes, Jane had also bought her toiletries and make-up.

For some considerable time, Carmen sat in front of the mirror applying then removing make-up. After some time in front of the mirror, she decided against wearing any for her meeting with Javi, as she did not want him to think she was making herself look attractive for him. She slung a jacket across her shoulders and hung the long thin strap of her new handbag over her right shoulder. Feeling satisfied with what she saw in the mirror, she went to meet up with Javi.

In the corner of the small common room, Javi sat alone at a walnut coffee table on which there was a bottle of red wine and two glasses, one of which was half full, the other empty.

'You look great. I didn't recognise you at first!' Javi said.

'Jane took me to get a new wardrobe this morning. I felt so trapped in those same clothes that I have worn day in, day out. It's strange how new clothes can give you a different sense of yourself. They have lots of clothes in the store. You should have a look.'

'Rachel is taking me tomorrow. Manuel, who I met last night, assured me that they will have clothes that will fit me. He also gave me a couple of bottles of good quality wine. Have a glass!'

'Oh, I'm not sure. I had a couple of glasses of wine last night and I suffered for it with a poor night's sleep.'

'Go on,' replied Javi, handing her a full glass that he had gone ahead and poured to the top before she had given her response.

'So many people worth meeting last night! And a few of them who are in the party. I'm meeting up with them at the end of the week. You should come along,' continued Javi.

'I've lost interest in politics. Anyhow I was never involved in the party, the way you were.'

'It could be a good thing for us to do together.'

'It sounds like something that would be good for you to do. I also met one or two people last night I liked. One of them wants to meet up with me and I might do that.'

'Nothing is good enough, is it?'

'What do you mean?'

'You don't want to spend any time with me now. We were together for almost a year before the coup. Remember that? Can't you at least tell me why your feelings for me have changed?'

'That time in prison, being in solitary confinement... So much has changed. Why are you angry with me? You know I get anxious when attacked like this,' she replied, as she got up to leave.

'Don't go, Carmen, please. Don't go! I'm sorry. I promise I won't get angry. The truth is I can't stand the thought of losing you,' he said, covering his face with both hands, his voice breaking as he fought back tears.

'Javi, I'm sorry. I'm still struggling to come to terms with what has happened. In fact so much so that I am considering taking the offer of counselling,' she said as she put her hand on his.

'You should if it's going to help you. Can't we just spend this evening reminiscing about the past, the good parts, that is?'

'Okay, but I haven't gone back that far for a very long time,' Carmen said, after a long pause.

For the next hour, Javi became ever more animated, telling stories involving characters and events that he insisted they both had in common. Most of those events and characters Carmen had trouble recalling, but on those she had recollections of, she made contributions based on such distant memories that they seemed to belong in another existence. As the evening wore on, she wondered why she had quite different recollections from those that Javi recounted, with an unremitting assurance that all that he was citing had been exactly as he described. That caused Carmen to worry whether her memory was functioning as it should and whether she had suffered some form of brain damage when in captivity.

Despite the struggle to recall much of what Javi was describing, by the time the bottle of wine was finished Carmen had relaxed into a state of listening without intervening in the stories that may or may not have been as Javi insisted. The stories posed no threat to her, and she was content to stay when Javi returned with another bottle; his enthusiasm for talking of the past undiminished.

'Being given so much wine shows how popular you must have already become, Javi, even though you have only been here for a few days.'

'I certainly think Rachel likes me. In fact, I reckon she is physically attracted to me,' said Javi as he proceeded to pour the wine right up to the brim of both glasses.

'What makes you think that?'

'She smiles at me a lot and she's attentive to me and wants to be in my company so much of the time.'

'Isn't she just doing her job?'

'I don't think so. Some things are the same the world over.'

'How can you be so sure? You wouldn't want to get something like that wrong, would you?'

Javi shrugged and smiled. He returned to telling more

stories from the past fuelled by the wine. On completing the second bottle of wine, which he had drunk entirely on his own, Carmen suggested that they end the evening at that.

'Well, if you are not up for any more wine, how about a coffee to finish off? Your room or mine? A good way to end the evening,' Javi said.

'Okay, I can do coffee in my room. But just the one. I'm tired and have to get to bed.'

As they sat around the coffee table in Carmen's room, Javi was now silent. At first he stared at the floor, but then started running his eyes over Carmen, from her face to her breasts, and down to her legs and feet.

'I'm really tired. We can do this again some other time, but I need my sleep now,' Carmen said, as she stood up and made her way past him to open the door to see him out. All of a sudden, Javi was on his feet. As she was passing him, he pulled her towards him and started to kiss her. Unable to free herself from his hold, she pulled her face away from him and stretched her head backwards as far as she could, to stop him reaching her lips. He stretched out his hand and with full force pulled her head towards him.

'Don't! You're scaring me,' pleaded Carmen.

'How? I'm not being angry, I'm being affectionate. You never used to object to this.'

'Let me go!' Carmen said in a raised voice, trying hard to pull herself free of his hold.

Javi stopped smiling, strengthened his grip and pulled her towards the bed with enough force to overcome what strength she had to resist.

'Don't!' screamed Carmen.

He pressed his hand over her mouth and pushed her onto the bed and straddled her, pinning her head down with his left hand, as he pushed his right hand inside her top. She applied all her strength to push him off, but couldn't free herself from under his weight, so she struck out with her fists. In the struggle, his hand slipped, enabling her to bite hard into one of his fingers that was pressing on her mouth. He pulled his hand away, shaking it in pain while she screamed with all the effort she could manage. Panic came over him. He feared her piercing screams would be causing alarm. Desperate to get out and away, he stumbled off the bed and struggled with the doorknob, before throwing the door open and rushing down the corridor, through the exit door and into the night.

The disturbance caused Dolores to come running out of her room a little further down the hallway. She came to a sudden halt in front of the half-open door of Carmen's room, from which there was now no sound. She tentatively pushed the door open, to see Carmen on the bed lying with her knees pulled up to her chest, rocking backwards and forwards while staring at the ceiling. Dolores approached the bed, leaned over and took hold of her, gently stroking her head.

'Carmen, are you hurt? What happened?'

Carmen did not respond but released her tight hold of the pillow and reached out to take hold of Dolores' hand. It was several minutes before her grip relaxed.

'Do you want a glass of water or a coffee?' asked Dolores.

'Water, please.'

Dolores brought her a glass of water which Carmen sat up to take hold of.

'Do you want me to call your support worker? I think I should call someone.'

'No, don't, please!'

'I caught a glimpse of a man running out of the building. Did someone attack you?'

'No. Not like before.'

'What do you mean?'

'Nothing.'

'Someone attacked you? Who was it?'

'I'd rather not say. I'm not hurt.'

'I think you should talk to someone about this. You've had a terrifying experience. I'll stay here with you until the morning.'

'Thank you. You've been so kind, Dolores, but honestly, I'll be okay on my own with the door locked. He won't come back now. I promise I will talk to Jane tomorrow.'

'If that's what you want. If you change your mind and need me, then shout or knock on my door, whatever the time.'

'Thanks, Dolores. I'll see to you in the morning. I'll be fine now.'

Javi locked his door behind him, still breathing hard. He poured himself a glass of water and noticed that his hands were shaking. After drinking it down in one go, he filled the glass up again and drank some more. He sat on his bed and put his head in his hands. He felt nauseous. He hadn't struck her, had he? No! He had let go of her when it was clear that she did not want to have sex. What could he be blamed for then? There was nothing he had done, other than misunderstand the situation. She had been so friendly towards him, in the way she used to be when they were in love in Chile. Hadn't she put her hand on his? And hadn't she invited him back to her room for coffee? Why had she led him on like that?

No wonder he had got it wrong. He would apologise to her and that would be the end of the matter, he told himself, as he undressed and got into bed. He lay awake for more than an hour, unable to get her terrified screaming out of his head. He had never seen her like that before. No matter how hard he tried to rationalise what he had done, the sense of unease would not recede. After a while worrying about possible repercussions, he fell asleep.

Carmen sat bolt upright, pressed against the headboard of her bed. For the first time, she had been unable to stop her mind going over every detail of that first rape in prison. It had swept over her like a massive wave and overcome all of her attempts to resist. Memories now flooded out from what had been a tightly secured fortress deep in her unconscious. Images of terror. Being punched and kicked without mercy. Struggling to breathe under the suffocating weight of the prison guard. Trying to avoid his mouth on her lips. Being unable to escape his foul breath. Of having to bear his insults and his mocking laughter. Lying traumatised and semi-conscious on the floor of the cell, at the end of it.

The aftermath of that first rape was now vivid in her mind. The gnawing pain that remained for days after. The repulsion of having been violated and beaten. How bereft and unprotected she'd felt. The hours weeping on the prison-cell floor with only a dirty blanket to stave off the cold. The hopeless exhaustion that she could not throw off for days on end. And that longing to die, yet knowing she could not manage to kill herself, despite the fear that at any time they could return to do it all again to her. It had all come back to her. Then another wave surged as she began thinking of the rapes that had followed. How every time she had fought until overcome by brutal force. Being beaten. Losing consciousness. Waking up to realise that this was a nightmare from which there was no escape. Then she remembered it. Spreading her own excrement over her body. It had worked – the guards kept away from her after that.

For some time, Carmen remained rigid and upright on her bed, tears trickling down her cheeks. It was as if she had come through a violent episode of vomiting, rendering her powerless to stop what was being expelled from her body. She was left with that exhausted relief of having survived what had so violently taken hold of her. As the darkness began turning to twilight, she got up to make herself a cup of coffee. As she sat holding the hot drink in her cupped hands, she knew that all was now different. Never again would she continue to conceal this pain and terror. She would see Jane in the morning and tell her everything.

Chapter 4

There was a gentle tapping on the door. Jane drank the last of her coffee, before getting up from her desk to open the door. Carmen stood on the doorstep looking pale and drawn, her eyes red and bloodshot. Jane thought back to when they had first met at the airport and her heart dropped.

'Carmen, come in! Take a seat at the coffee table over there. Do you want something to drink?'

'Water will be fine, thanks.'

As soon as Carmen had taken a sip of water, she started to tell her story. She recounted everything that had occurred with Javi the previous evening.

'I am so sorry. We'll move you to somewhere you feel safe.'

'If you could, I'd very much appreciate that. But that's only the start of what I need to tell you. There's a lot more... much worse.'

Without allowing Jane any time to respond, she began to describe all that she had endured while in captivity. She gave a sometimes hesitant but detailed account of the first rape and its aftermath. She stopped briefly to wipe her eyes and take a few deep breaths in order to steady her voice. It was at this point that Jane took hold of Carmen's hand. Carmen continued her account of the further rapes that she had been subject to and the broken state she had ended up in. Now there would be no more concealment. She then fell silent with her head bowed. Carmen began to sob and at that point Jane put her arm around her shoulders, trying her hardest to not break down herself.

'Oh Carmen! What endurance you must have to have survived that. I will do all that I can to help you get through this. And you will get through it, I promise.'

'I feel relief that I don't have to keep it a secret any longer. I don't know how I managed to keep it all submerged for so long. I now realise that's not good for me – not for my health, not for my future.'

'You've been living in a state of prolonged trauma, but as you say, you're now facing up to it. It's the start of your recovery, Carmen. I honestly believe that.'

'I hope so. I know I am a long way from getting back to how I was and leading a normal healthy life again, but I am beginning to think that what I thought was impossible, may not be now.'

'Anyone who has been through what you have, needs help. You can't do recovery on your own. I can arrange the counselling I mentioned previously – if you agree of course.'

'Yes. I want to try that now. I'd be grateful if you could arrange that.'

Jane suggested that before she started the counselling, Carmen should first see a doctor. She told Carmen of a female doctor who would give her a full health examination to see how she was physically, and then assess whether she needed any medication, given the horrendous physical and mental abuse she had suffered. Carmen agreed. Jane stated it would be best if she did not take on the role of counsellor but remained in her present role of supporting Carmen through this next stage and helping with all the other matters she would need to deal with to get on with building a new life.

'Does that make sense?' Jane asked.

'Yes, it does, but I have no money to pay for counselling. Will I be given information on the counsellors you have in mind and have a say in choosing?'

'As for the cost, don't worry. That will all be taken care of and yes, you will make the decision on choice of counsellor.'

'Thanks, Jane. I'm so grateful.'

'The other thing which you need to make a decision on is Javi. Do you want us to contact the police? I'll do that if you want and support you through the process.'

Carmen replied that she didn't want to get the police involved. Javi wasn't the one who had raped her after all. What he did was wrong, aggravated by him getting drunk, but she had no motivation to punish him. Nevertheless, she'd prefer not to see him, certainly not while she was having counselling. However, she would like to move to a place where she wouldn't have to worry about bumping into him.

'If you are sure that you don't want the police involved then that's how it will be. We can move you somewhere more suitable, but it will involve sharing with others as it's not possible to get a flat of your own – at least not for a while yet. Is there anyone you would be happy to share with?'

'Isabel Villegas. I met her the other night at the welcome event. I know she lives in a flat with her partner so she may not be able to have me there. The only other person that comes to mind is Dolores. She was so kind to me last night. I trust her.'

'I'll talk to Isabel. She and Pablo have a two-bed flat. I won't say anything other than you are feeling anxious with so many people around. Dolores is a lovely person but moving in with her would not get you out of the place where Javi is also living. I'll get this fixed one way or the other by the end of the day.'

'Thank you, Jane.'

In the early evening, Jane drove Carmen to the flat that Isabel shared with Pablo.

'Welcome, Carmen. You can stay with us for as long as you want. Let me show you your room, which I think you will like.'

'This is so kind of you and Pablo. He's okay with me being here?'

'Of course he is. I'll show you to your room and if you want to have a shower, feel free. I am cooking and we can eat at seven if that is okay. Pablo is working this evening and won't be back until late.'

Carmen closed the door of her room, sat down on the bed and surveyed the room. Although smaller than what she'd had in the halls of residence, it was the first time since leaving Chile that the accommodation felt like home. She put that down to the furnishings: a thick pile rug on the floor, a couple of framed impressionist prints on the walls, two pots of flowering geraniums on the windowsill and a bookcase full of books, most in English but a few in Castellano. She wasted no time in unpacking her clothes into the wardrobe and the chest of drawers and then taking a long, restful shower. Some considerable time was spent choosing what to wear for dinner. Before opening her bedroom door to go to dinner, she stopped and surveyed her room and allowed herself a satisfied smile.

The table was laid with a single candle in the centre that caused flickering shadows on the walls. Two places had been set and a bottle of red wine was uncorked.

'That's a bottle of good Chilean wine. I have cooked a cazuela from home, so I hope that's fine with you,' said Isabel as she handed Carmen a glass of wine.

'Sound's great!'

'A toast that you will feel at home here with Pablo and me. Please stay with us for as long as you want, Carmen.'

'I'm so grateful to you all; you, Pablo, and Jane, of course.'

'Jane is such a kind person, as far as all our people here are concerned. She's always so calm and patient and will do everything she can for any one of us. You're fortunate that she's your support worker.'

'I realise that,' replied Carmen.

Over the meal, Isabel told Carmen all about Clifton, the area of the city in which the flat was located and listed the local amenities that were within walking distance. She then spoke of when she and Pablo had arrived in Bristol and those first few months of getting acclimatised to somewhere that was so strange for them. Bit by bit they had begun to feel secure, but that stage then brought on a period of guilt when thinking of the others who had not managed to escape the violence and torture of the dictatorship.

Both Pablo and Isabel could speak some English when they'd arrived but in the first few months they had worked hard in an intensive course to improve. Isabel explained that by the end of the course they were able to engage in English conversation in most situations, which meant that they could communicate and engage with the local community. That was the important breakthrough, according to Isabel, and it had since led to opportunities where Pablo got a job and Isabel could take up the training opportunities she wanted to follow. Pablo was finding his job both enjoyable and rewarding. Isabel was about to start her social work training course.

'And what about you, Carmen? What are you planning to do?'

'Well, I've not long been here. I'm just happy to be in England. As to the future, I'm not sure yet, but perhaps teaching Spanish. I was thinking of becoming a schoolteacher before the coup put paid to that idea. But first, I need to get some personal things sorted.'

Carmen related the trauma of her captivity in considerable

detail and why staying at the hall of residence was now not what she could cope with.

'Oh Carmen! I suspected that something horrendous had happened to you, but never anything as bad as that. Anything we can do to help you, please just say. This is your home now and I promise it will be a place where you will always feel safe and welcome.'

'When I first met you the other night, I knew right away that you were someone I could trust. You stood out for picking up on the state I was in, but you did not push me to talk. Thank you. There is something you could help me with, but I feel a bit nervous about asking.'

'Don't be nervous, Carmen. I want to help in any way I can.'

Carmen recounted how on the previous night she had got herself into a mess with Javi. She explained their relationship before fleeing Chile and how it had changed following captivity. After all that Carmen had gone through, she had lost any desire to be with him – certainly not to be intimate with him. She couldn't bring herself to tell him of the rapes, so he still didn't know why things had changed between them. Last night they had spent some time alone together for the first time since leaving Chile, which was fine until he came on strong and was intent on having sex.

'He's not the problem but I don't want him near me while I am getting help, and I don't want him to try to seek me out or contact me. Could you, or Pablo, let him know that?'

'Yes. I'm sure we can do that. I'll talk to Pablo tonight when he gets back. We will agree with you which one of us should speak to Javi and what we should say to him.'

'Thank you. I'm already feeling much better than I was when we first met. Probably because I've made the decision to face up to the mess I am in.'

49

'Come here, Carmen. I don't know about you, but I need a hug. Everything is going to work out for you. I'm sure of it.'

Later, after Carmen had gone to bed, Pablo arrived home to find Isabel waiting up for him. She told him everything of the conversation with Carmen. He listened without interrupting and after Isabel had finished he sat with his forearms on his knees, staring at the floor.

'What are you thinking?' Isabel asked.

'I'm just thinking how terrifying it must have been for her. How difficult it must have been for her just to survive that, never mind get over it and pick up her life again. Poor woman. What about you; how are you?'

'I'm shocked. Indeed, how does a woman recover from something like that? What I do know is that we must do what we can to help her. What about this matter with Javi?'

'I'll speak to him. I think I should do that. If he still doesn't know what happened to Carmen. how is he to understand what has happened between them and why he should comply with her wish to be left alone?'

'He frightened her, so I'm not that concerned with how he is feeling.'

'I'm not excusing his behaviour. I'm just pointing out that if he is not to bother her as she wants, then he is far more likely to do that if told of the terrible things that she has been subjected to. And remember, he is also a refugee alone in a strange country where he has just arrived. He needs a bit of help and understanding too.'

'Okay, but Carmen has to decide how this is to be handled. It's not for us to make that decision.'

'Will you talk to her, or should we do it together?'

'We should do it together. She needs to feel comfortable with both of us given she is going to be living here. We'll do it tomorrow.'

The medical examination which Jane had arranged resulted in Carmen being prescribed a course of Valium to relieve stress and she was also prescribed antibiotics for gonorrhoea, which she had been suffering from since her time in captivity. By the time of the meeting in the evening with Isabel and Pablo, the effects of the Valium had already kicked in. She listened to Pablo's reasons for telling Javi about what had happened in captivity and did not intervene until he had finished.

'I never wanted to be the person telling him about those things, but yes, it would be best if he knew. And you're right that he is more likely to comply with my request for no contact if he knows what happened to me.'

'I'll make it clear that no contact means no contact, until you say otherwise. Is it okay to put it in that way?' Pablo asked.

'Yes. I don't mind if he wants to contact you or Isabel to find out how I am, but I don't want him to contact me directly.'

'Of course! I'll tell him what you have said and make it clear that he must not bother you, especially during this counselling period and until you say otherwise.'

Carmen found it difficult to be decisive when choosing a counsellor from the list that Jane had put together, but she opted for a counsellor called Becky Arnold, simply because she had worked with other refugees, not only Chilean refugees, but with women refugees from other countries, some of whom had been raped. Walking down the hillside avenue to her first counselling session, Carmen was warmed by the afternoon sunshine and found herself wondering for the first time what occurred in a counselling session. Would she be asked a lot of questions? Would she have to lie on a couch? The image of her lying on a chaise longue made her smile and she shook her head at the thought of being asked to.

She arrived at the address and walked up the driveway to the weathered, unvarnished door of a white, detached Georgian house. She was shown into the waiting room where a middle-aged woman waiting to be seen gave her a cursory smile before returning to read the magazine she had on her lap. Carmen began to feel anxious so to distract herself she picked up a magazine from a bundle that lay on the coffee table. However, she could not work up sufficient focus to read so she browsed through the pictures instead. After what she considered to be an undue length of time, she heard her name being called by a woman, who was standing in the doorway at the end of the room. The woman looked only a few years older than she was and smiled at her.

'Carmen Rodriguez?' she repeated.

Carmen rose from her seat without saying anything.

'I'm Becky Arnold. Come through.'

Carmen sat down in one of the leather easy chairs on either side of an oval coffee table and turned down the offer of a tea or coffee, preferring to stick with the glass of water on the table. Becky set out her qualifications and experience of providing counselling services and then gave a brief outline of the process and the aims of counselling, stressing that she did not have a rigid approach, but that she was first and foremost, interested in helping Carmen with the difficulties she was having in coping with the aftermath, and only going into any detail about the rapes if and when Carmen wanted to do that. She asked what medication Carmen was on and when told she responded that one of the target outcomes of the counselling would be for her to reach a point where she would have no need of Valium, hopefully well before the counselling course was complete. She then asked Carmen to set out what had happened to her.

Becky brought the first session to a close, complimenting her on her courage and fortitude and expressing the view that this was a good start and she was certain that Carmen would in time recover from the trauma she had been living with for so long. She suggested that at the next session Carmen could talk in more detail about how to best manage anxiety. It was suggested to her that keeping a journal, detailing the occasions when she felt anxious, would help. If she could bring those to the sessions, it would allow them together to explore ways to reduce the frequency and intensity of the anxiety attacks. Carmen nodded.

On her way back home, she was drained of all energy, although relieved at how well the first session had gone. Carmen was convinced that Becky was a person she could confide in; someone who made her feel comfortable in opening up about the pain and anguish she had kept secret for so long. This had been a good start and although she had some way to go, there would be no going back to the state she had been locked into for so long.

Javi sat with his head in his hands. He was trying to come to terms with what Pablo had just told him.

'I had no idea. We were lovers when we fled our homeland together, so why could she not have told me of those terrible things?'

'I can't talk for someone who has been through what Carmen has. There is so much she herself can't make sense of. I can understand why this is so difficult for you, Javi. It would be for anyone in this situation,' replied Pablo.

'After all we have been through – fleeing our homeland, our families and so many friends. Then this! I am struggling to cope with it. I must have failed her given that she wasn't able to confide in me.'

'Carmen needs space and time to get well. Recovery is not guaranteed given what she has been through. I am sure that

Manuel and some of those people you met the other night will help you through this.'

'Why would anyone want to help me, given what I have done. I feel like I am cursed.'

'We have all been cursed, Javi, but we are still the fortunate ones in having survived. This may be a low point, but things will get better for you.'

'You can tell her she needn't worry about me contacting her directly. Do you think she will recover from all she has been through?'

'I really don't know.'

Chapter 5

Shortly after starting the counselling, Dolores suggested to Carmen that she join her on her daily walk on the Clifton Downs. Carmen's first reaction was one of reluctance, but Dolores persuaded her to try it. After the first one Carmen then began to look forward to their frequent walks and chats. Dolores had a specific interest in fauna and flora and had built up a knowledge of the wildflowers to be found on the Downs and on the crags tumbling down to the muddy river below.

'Dolores, how do you know so much about everything that is growing here?'

'I have been reading up about the plants and shrubs that grow on the Downs now that I have a job in the botanical gardens. I have always had a strong attachment to nature, perhaps because I have Aymara blood on my father's side. Have you heard of Pachamama?'

'I've heard the term, but I'm not exactly sure of what it is.'

'Pachamama is Mother Earth for the Indigenous people of the Andes such as the Aymara. Everything that grows, indeed the fertility of the earth, is down to the goddess. My father taught me how sacred nature is even though we lived far from it in the industrial city of Antofagasta and the only work he could get was at the docks exporting nitrates which he considered stolen goods from the earth, up north in the Atacama Desert.'

'That must have been hard for him, living and working in such an urban environment.'

'It was, but at least he didn't lose his life as his grandfather did in the massacre in Iquique of the nitrate workers and their families, about seventy years ago. Do you know about the strike there and how the Government and mine owners massacred over two thousands of men, women and children? Many Chileans don't, as it was kept secret for many years after.'

'Yes, I do know of it, but it wasn't something I learned at school but through my political activism. You and your family must have lived through so much hardship.'

'I don't think I have much to complain about compared with others, including you, Carmen. Maybe I should put my good fortune down to Pachamama.'

'So that's why you are so positive about life?'

'Perhaps. You have to remember that Pachamama is Mother Earth. She's not Mother Chile. I can commune with nature here as much as I can in Chile. That's maybe why I have less of a sense of loss than others in exile.'

Dolores' sharing of her knowledge and enthusiasm for wildflowers distracted Carmen from any thoughts of counselling and from dwelling on the reasons why she was doing it. It was not long before Carmen herself was searching for and identifying some of the wildflowers that Dolores had told her of, such as Honeywort and Allium. Besides the feel-good factor brought on by the variety of colour, in particular the blues, reds and whites that seemed to sparkle amid the lighter and darker shades of green foliage, Carmen was intoxicated by the range of scents. It was as if she had rediscovered long-lost senses and after those first walks on the Downs she realised that immersing herself in the natural world gave her a vibrancy and lightness that had been lost to her.

Several weeks before completing her counselling sessions, Carmen stopped taking Valium and slept through the night without waking up. That had not happened since prior to the coup almost two years ago. Throughout this stage of recovery, Carmen had also been meeting up with Jane to explore options for work and accommodation and a plan had been put together for her future. This included an imminent move to her own flat around the beginning of September, then starting a teacher-training course in October, with the intention of qualifying as a Spanish teacher and finding a job in one of the city's schools, the following year.

By the end of August, the counselling sessions were at an end. Carmen was confident that there would be no return of the trauma which she had been trapped in for so long. There was no denial of the memory of all the brutality she had suffered, nor of the pain and humiliation that could still arise from time to time, but she now had the awareness to spot anxiety at the initial stages and was well practised in what she had to do to manage it.

There was one other matter that Carmen wanted to resolve so she decided to write to Javi. She set out an explanation of how her mental health had deteriorated as a consequence of her time in captivity and all that happened there, and to assure him that having completed the counselling, she was now feeling so much better about herself and had a growing optimism for the future. She now wished to move on from their relationship, particularly how it had ended, but she would be happy to meet up with him as she would any of her friends, of which he was one. A couple of weeks after she had sent the letter, no reply had been received.

'Isabel, I've not had a response from Javi to my letter. It's not causing me a big problem, but I would prefer if it was all resolved between us.'

'Pablo sees him from time to time. Perhaps I shouldn't be the one to tell you this, but he has a girlfriend now. She's English – Rachel, the woman who was his support worker. Maybe that's the reason he hasn't responded to your letter.'

'Really? That didn't take him long. I suppose it's welcome news as it shows he accepts that we are no longer in a relationship.'

'And how does that make you feel?'

'Recently, I have found myself thinking back to the times we had in Chile. We had our ups and downs right up to the time of the coup, but that threw us together with an intensity that was not there before. Continuing the relationship was all bound up with the coup rather than a deep love – certainly on my part.'

'So what now, Carmen?'

'It's all in the past for me and I don't just mean Javi, but my life and times in Chile before the coup. I don't have a strong attachment to the past like others have. I miss my mother and brother certainly, and I long for the time when I can see them again. But I feel adrift from my past life in Chile now.'

'You do seem much less attached to the past than the rest of us and more focused on what the future may bring.'

'Don't get me wrong, I'll celebrate when Chile returns to democratic government and when we can all go back there in safety if we want to, but god knows if and when that will ever happen. I just feel that I should focus on my life in the here and now, and not spend so much time inside my head, which is where the past resides.'

'Yes, it's important to focus on the present, but there are still times when I feel like I am caught in a sort of limbo, frozen between what happened before and some uncertain future. I can find myself missing many of the pleasures of simply experiencing what life throws up.'

Carmen was no longer sure how much of the past happened as one can often be convinced it did, because of how the mind can play tricks when reminiscing. She cited as an example the evening she spent with Javi when he behaved badly. He had talked about the past in Chile yet she could not remember a lot of the scenes, events, or people, being as he claimed they were. She couldn't make up her mind how much she had forgotten, not noticed, or got wrong way back then; or how much Javi was imagining or intentionally making up about the past, because that is how he wanted it to be.

'It's best not to spend too much time reminiscing as without noticing it, one can start to treat life as something simply to look back on,' replied Isabel.

'My time living here with you and Pablo is about to come to an end, but I will never forget it. You will remain treasured friends throughout the rest of my life. I am sure of that.'

'Well, you're right about one thing! You're not going to get rid of us easily.'

Javi sat by the fireside with a glass of red wine in his hand and a near-empty wine bottle on the coffee table next to Carmen's letter, which he had taken out of his jacket pocket to read yet again, as he had so many times since its arrival almost two weeks ago. He had told no one that he had received it, not even Rachel with whom he had just made love and who was asleep in the next room. In the weeks following his flight from Carmen's room in the halls of residence, so alarmed had he been by her distressed screaming, he had veered from being overcome with guilt that he had caused her such upset, to anger at her failure to confide in him. At times he was convinced that she was to blame for him behaving as he had.

Shortly after the humiliating day when Pablo had come to tell him about the rapes and assaults on her when in captivity,

Javi had felt intense shame; not only about others knowing of his behaviour that drunken night but also having failed to have worked out the cause of her changed behaviour towards him, which in retrospect seemed so obvious. He then put the whole matter behind him. Since that decision, he had not attempted to communicate with Carmen nor sought to find out from Pablo how she was.

His first-class degree in Chemistry from Santiago University had enabled him to gain a teaching post at Bristol University, and in the last few weeks he had been busy preparing for the start of term in early October. In the previous couple of months, he also poured a lot of his time into attending meetings with other Chileans, either discussing politics or socialising with them. There were endless discussions on politics and sometimes heated disagreements about the failures and successes of the Allende Government. Those were welcome and restored his self-esteem, by making him forget what had happened in his relationship with Carmen, when he had ended up being rejected by a woman for the first time.

Out of those political discussions and socialising with other party members had come the idea of establishing a monthly newsletter for Chilean refugees in England. He had offered to help undertake this and had spent the last few weeks editing and producing the first issue with Manuel. It had been published at the beginning of the week and that was also a source of distraction from Carmen's letter. The other major development in his life was his relationship with Rachel. He considered that it had happened without much effort on his part, which he took as an indication that it would not last long but being in love with someone again felt invigorating. More than anything else, it made him feel good about himself and submerged those feelings of low esteem and despair that had followed what he saw as that shameful scene in Carmen's room.

Although he had moved in with Rachel, he had no expectations for the relationship. The principal reason was because a return to Chile was his priority, albeit he accepted that would not be imminent.

The letter from Carmen had aroused a mixture of feelings, but in the main it made him feel irritated that he had to deal with something that he had hoped was buried in the past. He thought about not responding but decided that such a course of inaction was likely to mean he would never be free of the matter, and that option would also require him to always be careful to avoid situations where he might meet her. He was fretting about what was best to do to resolve this unwelcome problem in his otherwise promising life, when on checking his watch, he saw that it was time for him to be on his way to the political meeting, held every alternate Friday evening in a back room in a pub in Clifton. Picking up Carmen's letter from the table, he put it back carefully in its envelope and slipped it into his inside pocket. He did not wake Rachel before leaving for the pub.

On the way to the meeting, he resolved to end any further prevarication and write a letter to Carmen in response to hers. It would be set in a positive tone and would emphasise his relief and happiness that she was feeling better. There would be no engagement as to why she had not confided in him about the rapes, which he now considered the main cause for their relationship being at an end. As to meeting up with her, he would suggest that would best be done in a group setting, such as a party meeting, feeling sure that she would never want to attend such a gathering. He would conclude the letter by informing her of his relationship with Rachel and that he wished Carmen well for the future. The next day he drafted the letter and sent it to the address he had for Pablo.

Chapter 6

It was late February 1976 when Pablo walked home in the early hours of the still dark morning, having completed his first nightshift at the psychiatric hospital. He hoped that would be the last time he had to work a nightshift. He had been asked to work overnight due to the high levels of staff sickness at the hospital. There was nothing he had enjoyed about it. He could find little to occupy himself with during the never-ending night, due to the absence of any engagement with patients. He had fallen into a state of mind which he knew should be avoided at all costs, as it always left him unsettled and then agitated for some time after.

Sitting alone in the ward office, he had gone back in time; to events of the day of the coup, the terror and beatings of long interrogations, the flight from his homeland and the loss of family and friends, left behind in that land he was now exiled from. By the time his shift finished at six in the morning, he had been sucked into a deep despair that he knew would hang over him now for a week or even longer.

He walked home as there were few buses at that time of the very early morning. The absence of traffic on the streets began to distract him from his deteriorating mood and before long he found himself taking long, deep inhalations of the chilled and refreshing air that he had never experienced before in the city. It was still some time from dawn breaking, and he became enthralled by the range and the volume of birdsong in the trees and bushes that he was strolling by. Do birds sing as much and at such a volume in the daytime, he asked himself. Perhaps they might well do, but were never heard, drowned out by traffic and industrial noise that was absent from the sleeping-city night. He began to whistle as he strolled home in the dark and empty streets. The onset of drizzling rain started to return him to despair and by the time he arrived home, he was soaked in a deep sense of loss, for past times, places and the loved ones he feared he would never see again.

As he opened the front door, Isabel came to mind. She must not see him in this state and it wouldn't be long before she awoke, as dawn was now breaking. Wasn't there something he could do to escape the worst of a deep depression? Tiredness prevented him embarking on anything that required an intensive level of energy so he slumped into a chair, placed his forearms on the kitchen table and laid his head down intending to fall asleep. Yet he was unable to drift off to sleep due to his mind ticking over, attempting to find some way to pull himself out of depression after he awoke.

Working overnight had made him feel queasy so he had no wish to have breakfast. All of a sudden he got up from the table and started to make breakfast in bed for Isabel. By the time he made his way to the bedroom door, concentrating on carrying the full breakfast tray without spilling anything, his depression had been left behind.

'Your breakfast is served, madam. Coffee, toast and jam, as has become your preference.'

Isabel opened her eyes and as she slowly sat up, a smile spread over her face.

'It's good to have a lover who tends to my every need, even at such an early hour,' Isabel said as she rubbed sleep from her eyes.

'Your every need?'

'Well not every need, but certainly all those I could reasonably expect to have satisfied by a man.'

'Thank god for that. It would make me highly anxious if I had to tend to all your needs. Anyhow, what would those needs be that you don't look to me for?'

'The ones that can only be realised with my women friends. You know – intelligent conversation about feelings and health issues, being supportive and interested in each other's thoughts and concerns, joking about how strange men are… things like that.'

'Women can be strange too, you know. Take those older, female nursing staff at work! They get really worked up if the sheets and blankets on beds haven't been squared the way they demand. Now that you mention your women friends, how is Carmen doing?'

'Last night when I went round there, I noticed that she doesn't avoid talking about all the harrowing things while held in captivity. She doesn't get herself into that distressed state that she was constantly in shortly after her arrival. The first time I met her, I was left worrying how such a fragile person was ever going to survive.'

'She's clearly in a better place, although she will probably never forget the trauma. Has she started the teacher training course?'

'Just last week, and she's coping well – even said she enjoys it. She also mentioned that she had finally got a response from Javi to her letter. She believes that his response means both of them can move on with their lives now. He even told her of his new relationship with Rachel. What do you make of him?'

Pablo explained that he had seen him last week and he seemed happy with his life now, with his new job and a new woman. He had also become highly active on the political front.

'I know you don't like him, but I am loathe to be critical of anyone who has had to flee their country, their family, and their friends and then forced to build a life anew in a very different place, on the other side of the world,' Pablo said.

'I don't like him, you're right about that. I accept that he has been through a lot, like the rest of us, but being a refugee does not bestow immunity from judgement of character. He's not the man that you are.'

'He is very intelligent though or he wouldn't have got that lecturer's job at the university.'

'Academically perhaps, but not emotionally. If he had emotional intelligence, then he would have worked out that something horrendous had been inflicted on Carmen while in captivity. Instead, he claims he had no idea, or so he says.'

'Perhaps, but he's not so different from most men in that regard. He's not the person who raped her, remember.'

'I've already acknowledged that. All I am saying is that he is not well endowed when it comes to being sensitive to how others are, women in particular.'

'Am I well-endowed in that regard?'

'Much better than most men I would say but that's nothing to get carried away about. Of course, I don't just like you because of your character. You look like you need cheering up so why not get into bed. Anything the matter?'

'No, not really, well there is something. There was so little to do on the nightshift that I spent most of the night thinking about the past and getting myself into a miserable state again.'

'Oh Pablo! You can't keep being brought down like that. We are lucky to be here, lucky to have survived when so many haven't. We need to focus on a future for ourselves in the time and place we are living now.'

'You're right. I should try harder to keep in mind the plight of others who have had much worse things to deal with than I have.'

For some time, Isabel had been concerned about Pablo's tendency to not only get depressed but due to his unrealistic optimism that exile would end in the near future. He had not said anything to Isabel for a while about his belief that exile would soon be over, but he had turned down the offer by the hospital management to fund him to become a qualified psychiatric nurse. His rationale had been that given a return to Chile would happen in the near future, he could not in all honesty promise the hospital authorities that he would fulfil the obligation to work at the hospital during his training and for at least two years after qualifying. He cited the same reason for not getting married and for delaying having children until their exile came to an end.

Isabel had said nothing in response, such was his conviction that they would soon be returning to Chile. She was tired of challenging him to present the evidence that a return to Chile would happen anytime in the near future. He always smiled at that but never responded to the question. Isabel talked to some of her female friends about her concerns and they suggested that perhaps Pablo was just more of an optimist than the rest of them, as they knew no one else living here who held such a view.

She raised the matter with Manuel who had become Pablo's best friend.

'Is Pablo so different from any other Chilean who wants quick end to the dictatorship to enable a return home?' asked Manuel.

'It's not so much a case of him being optimistic but more one of compulsive denial. He also gets very depressed, often for weeks on end. I don't know what to do.'

'I didn't know he got depressed.'

'He wouldn't tell you that. It's one of his secrets.'

'It won't continue like that for ever. As time passes his

longing for a return to a lost life in Chile will begin to ebb away, simply because new experiences and attachments start to come to the fore of one's life.'

The conversation with Manuel left Isabel more reassured and she regained her optimism about their future together. However, Pablo's recurring depressions did not stop. When he fell into one, her worries would re-emerge, and she would try again to come up with something she could do to help Pablo move on from it. She never came up with anything that had much of an effect and had to settle on Manuel's advice of waiting for time to provide the solution, although she was never sure that would ever come to be.

Chapter 7

Isabel had not received a letter from her mother for over two weeks. She was accustomed to receiving one every week without fail during the last two years since settling in Bristol. On her return from work, she picked up a letter from the floor of the hallway and saw it was from Chile. The stamp always aroused excitement in her, but this time she noticed that it was not her mother's writing on the envelope but her sister Paula's.

On reading what her sister had written, the letter dropped from her hand into her lap. She gazed at the wall, seeing nothing. All colour drained away from her face, as a wailing erupted from deep inside, which brought Pablo running from the kitchen.

'Isabel, what's wrong?'

'She's dead... my mother is dead,' Isabel repeated several times. She did not respond to any of the other questions that Pablo asked. He cradled her in his arms, catching sight of the letter now lying on the floor by Isabel's feet. He leaned over to reach for it but decided it was not his to read. After a few minutes, Isabel bent down to pick up the letter from the floor and handed it to Pablo. She did not speak but gave a single nod to his question of whether she wanted him to read it. He took it from her hand, sat down next to her and began to read.

It had been six o'clock in the morning, when Paula was

awoken by loud banging on the front door and shouts from outside demanding that it be opened. On rushing downstairs she passed her mother who was sitting in her dressing gown on a chair with her head in her hands.

'They've come for me. I knew they would,' her mother said.

The door shuddered with every blow from the outside.

'We have to open the door, Mum, or they'll break it down.'

Her mother looked up at her and then nodded. Paula shouted out that she was opening the door. Four men dressed in black overalls, faces hidden by their balaclavas, burst through the doorway and pushed both of them up against the wall and searched them. Handcuffs were forced onto her mother's wrists.

'What are you doing? You can't do that to my mother.'

'Shut up you bitch or we'll take you as well.'

They pulled her mother up, almost lifting her off the floor. In a moment they were gone leaving the door wide open. Paula heard the vehicle doors being slammed, the ignition turning, then the screech of tyres as they sped away into the distance. Paula slumped down on the bottom stair and started to cry. After a few minutes, she got up and phoned her uncle. There was a long period of ringing. Just when she was about to put the phone down, he answered. Paula explained as best she could what had happened. He told her to stay put and that he would be around within fifteen minutes.

The early morning had been spent discussing what they should do with other close relatives whom her uncle had asked to come round to the house. They had agreed that Paula should phone the police, which she did only to be told that they had no information on any such incident that morning.

'Aren't you going to investigate? My mother has been abducted by masked men and you act as if you don't care,' Paula shouted down the phone.

'We will make inquiries and if we find out anything we will

contact you. Wait until we contact you,' said the officer before ending the call.

There was no further contact by mid-afternoon, so Paula and her uncle left the house to go down to the police station in the city centre. They demanded action and after refusing to leave the police station until they were told where her mother was, they were charged with obstruction and detained overnight. They were released the next day and told there would be no response to further questions until the police investigation into her mother's disappearance had been concluded.

Around midday on the second day after her abduction, a police officer called Paula to inform her that her mother had had a fatal heart attack while being questioned by DINA, the secret service, and despite being rushed to hospital, she had died before arriving there. Paula was still holding the receiver when she collapsed to the floor. She lay wailing for some time until she had the energy to drag herself up and phone her uncle. Accompanied by him and two aunts, she went to the hospital only to be told that the body had already been transferred to a funeral parlour. The coffin had been sealed. They were not allowed to view the body, despite pleading to do so.

They would never know what state DINA had left their mother in, but they had no doubt that the refusal to allow them to see the body was to conceal the maltreatment and torture they had inflicted. One of the two police officers present at the funeral parlour handed Paula a medical certificate stating the cause of death to be a heart attack and the time of death was 14:10hrs on 28 September 1976. The family asked to be allowed to arrange its own post-mortem, but this was denied, with the officer demanding that burial take place immediately as they had already provided a death certificate from the hospital doctor confirming the cause of death. Despite their objections, the burial took place the following day at the church near the funeral parlour, as insisted upon by the police. The police refused to grant the family's wish for her to be buried at her local church and interred in the local cemetery.

'Bastards!' Pablo said after reading the letter. Isabel did not respond and had her eyes fixed on the flames of the gas fire which Pablo had lit, after he had noticed that she was shivering. That had no effect so he had placed a blanket around her shoulders. Isabel shook her head when he asked if she wanted anything to eat or drink. They sat saying nothing with their arms around each other until Isabel broke the silence.

'I find it so hard to take in. She's been dead for the last two weeks and I didn't know. My mother died all alone in detention, without any of her family around her. God knows what suffering she went through. And I'm stuck here, thousands of miles away, unable to be where I should be – with my family.'

'That's hard to bear, but you mustn't punish yourself for being trapped in exile. I refuse to let the barbarity of the military defile the memory of your mother. I have nothing but positive memories of her. She was good to me, right from that first day you took me home to meet her and your sister.'

'She was a good person. I loved her so much. I can't bear it – the thought that I will never see her again,' Isabel said before falling again into a long silence, which Pablo knew was best left for her to decide when to end.

For the next week following the arrival of the letter Isabel thought of nothing but her mother. She took leave from her social-work course and after Pablo had left for work, she spent most of the first day of that week wandering alone through the rain-drenched streets of the city. Looking straight ahead and with no destination in mind, she walked past people as if they were not there, and on one or two occasions bumped into someone walking past her. Oblivious to the rain and chilly

71

wind, she walked for miles before arriving in a council housing estate on the outskirts of the city, where she had never been before.

She did not know where she was. The blocks of flats were uncared for, with rubbish strewn over the communal areas and grass verges. As she looked round, searching for a sign of where she was and how to get back home, she caught sight of an elderly woman approaching, who was struggling to walk, even with the aid of a walking stick.

'Are you lost, my love. Can I help?' asked the woman.

'I don't know where I am. I need to get to get back to Clifton where I live.'

'Come with me, my love, I'll take you to the bus stop. The buses are regular, so you won't have to wait long. Have you got money for the bus fare?'

Isabel shook her head, which prompted the woman to hand Isabel the walking stick and take her purse out of her handbag, from which she extracted a pound coin.

'Here, take this. I won a lot more than that at the bingo last night.'

Isabel took the pound coin and then handed the walking stick back to the old woman.

'The bus stop you need is just up there, on the other side of the road. You can't miss it. Get yourself home now, my love, and get out of those wet clothes or you'll catch your death,' said the woman as she waved goodbye with her raised walking stick and turned round to make her painful way to wherever she was going. Isabel stood at the bus stop soaked to the skin, waiting for the bus, but smiling for the first time since opening the letter from Chile. She could not stop thinking about the elderly woman. Did that really happen? she asked herself.

The next day she set off again through the streets of the city with a small backpack in which she had her purse, a notebook and a pen. There was a plan for the remainder of the week which was to recover every single memory of her mother that she could, arrange them in order and then write them all down. She would start with the earliest memories from her childhood, then move through her teenage years, into her adult life up to her flight from Chile with Pablo. During each day's wandering through the streets of Bristol she unearthed long-forgotten experiences and events. The day's memory-gathering would be brought to an end in her favourite café, drinking several coffees while sitting at a table on her own and writing in her notebook all that she had remembered from her wanderings. By the fifth day, she was unable to come up with any more memories and knew then that it was time to bring this grieving stage to an end.

Pablo arrived home from work to find the dinner table draped in a new table cover and two places set with their finest plates and cutlery, and several candles glowing in the otherwise dim room. Isabel had cooked a meal of empanadas and sopaipillas in the kitchen where Chilean music was being played. She had purchased two bottles of the best quality Chilean wine that she could find: one white and one red.

'I was going to suggest we go out and eat but this is a wonderful surprise,' said Pablo on seeing the table prepared like he had never seen it before.

'I thought we should have a wake to celebrate my mother's life and lay her to rest the only way I can, all these thousands of miles away. I will miss her for a long time, perhaps forever. I will think of her every day for the rest of my life.'

'Let's drink to her,' Pablo suggested.

'Start with the bottle of chardonnay chilling in the fridge,' replied Isabel.

After serving the meal that she had taken care to cook

to traditional Chilean recipes, she began to recount the last five days of wandering through the streets of the city, as if she had been searching them for memories of her mother, and how at the end of each day she had recorded what she had unearthed from her memory. For the first couple of days, she had been unable to come up with any memories of her mother other than feel-good ones and that had made her uneasy as it didn't constitute a true record of her relationship with her mother. Anything less than a full and honest account would feel dishonourable.

On the third day Isabel found herself being drawn into what started as a vague memory of when she was a young child. She had a feeling she had done something wrong, although she couldn't identify what that was. It was definitely something that would make her mother cross with her, if she ever found out. Her mother had asked her what was wrong, and she replied that she didn't like the man, a friend of her mother, who had become a frequent visitor to their home. Isabel had not responded to her mother's questions of why she didn't like him, and her mother showed some irritation with her as a result. A short time after, the man was never seen in the house again. All that remained was a memory of her mother in the kitchen sitting in silence with tears in her eyes, which made Isabel feel guilty that she had caused her mother to be so unhappy.

As the café came into sight where she would stop each day for coffee and write up her memories, a full recall surged to the forefront of her mind, as if a blockage in her memory had been removed. She saw the man touching her when they were alone in the house, which had made her feel confused and then frightened. Her mother had not suspected let alone realised this until Isabel blurted out her dislike for the man. That episode from her distant childhood, which had always been accompanied by unease without knowing why, all of a sudden had become clear, like the view of a hidden panorama after the fog had lifted. She remembered how a short time after the man disappeared from the house for good, her mother had taken her aside to tell her that she would never be cross with her for as long as she lived, as long as Isabel always told her if she were ever frightened of anyone, or of anything bad that had happened to her.

'Often, we suppress what we are too frightened to face up to. We prefer a past that is comfortable to live with. That's one reason why memory alone can never be a reliable tool for revealing the full reality of the past,' Isabel explained to Pablo, as she took another sip of wine.

'Yes, sometimes it is hard to be sure about all that did or did not happen in the past. Unconscious denial! I see it every day at work. Your mother acted decisively once she knew what was going on. You should think the best of her for that,' replied Pablo.

'I do. I'm still amazed at how that childhood memory remained hidden in my unconscious for so long.'

'Your mother would have smiled at any suggestion that you would ever hide from how things really are. You never accept anything that you hear or read without questioning it, and even some of what you see.'

'Yes, she taught us to always be wary of what we were told was fact, in particular what the media and the powers that be present as their version of how and why things are as they claim.'

'I love these stories of you and your mother. What else have you got in that notebook?'

Isabel opened it up and read aloud more of the events and scenes that she had managed to recall and write down. Isabel recalled how their mother had shown Isabel how to find ways to distract her younger sister when she was doing something annoying or disruptive. There were also memories of when Isabel was upset and angry with her mother for returning home sometimes more than an hour late from her work as a secondary school teacher. However, she could not recall a single instance of her mother showing irritation with her, although she felt sure there must have been at least a few occasions when her mother must have felt aggrieved, in particular when Isabel threw one of her many tantrums. At the close of that section in her notebook, she stated that her childhood had been a happy one, and that her single-parent mother was the principal reason for that.

In her teenage years, disagreements with her mother arose over what now seemed to be matters of little consequence. She started to keep secrets and be much less inclined to talk to her mother about what was happening in her life. She cited two examples of when she had not been forthcoming with her mother. The first when she lost her virginity aged sixteen and the other when she had shoplifted a few pairs of tights from a department store not long after. Several years later when Isabel told her mother of these events, she discovered that her mother had known of them all along. Although her mother was hurt at the time by Isabel not being honest, she had taken the view that her daughter would tell her in her own time. Both her mother's faith in her to be honest and her patient acceptance of Isabel's rites of passage had caused her to stop at a bench in a Bristol park to cry until she had no energy left.

The memories she had recorded from her early adult years were of her mother's growing political activity, in local as well as national issues. She took part in campaigns for better health services and the provision of accommodation for local homeless people, and also in demonstrations for restoring land rights and the provision of better services for the Mapuche Indian community. By that stage Isabel was also politically active and that compounded how close they had become again, after the distance of her teenage years.

Isabel finished her account of all she had written down in the last week by telling Pablo that there were many more stories to add, as she still had to sift through the hundreds of letters she had received from her mother down through the years. However, in the last five days, all she wanted to do was to let her memory bring back the past unaided, as it was more important to focus on remembering her mother rather than compiling some final account of all that had happened between them.

'It's a great idea to sift through all those letters between you and your mother then revise what you have written down these last five days. You could even produce a book as a memorial for yourself and your family.'

Isabel smiled at the suggestion.

'To your mother and how she brought you up to be who you are,' said Pablo as he raised his glass.

'The desolation has started to ebb a bit. What remains though is my anger and contempt for those who killed her. For as long as I live I will do what I can to expose those bastards for their brutality, but I will never let them contaminate the memory of how wonderful my mother was.'

Isabel smiled, got up from the table, and leaned over to give Pablo a long, passionate kiss.

'I think your mother must have been special too. Like mine, she must have taught you how to love,' Isabel whispered in Pablo's ear.

'Let's dance the Cueca in honour of our mothers,' said Pablo as he pulled Isabel into the kitchen where there was more room to dance. He put on a tape of traditional Chilean music, and they stood facing each other several feet apart to start the dance they both loved to do. She held her napkin aloft, while

Pablo placed one over his shoulder and clapped out the rhythm as they courted each other across the kitchen floor.

'Two things have rescued me. A brief encounter with an old woman living on a council estate, who did not hesitate to help someone in need she happened to come across. And second, your attention and patience. There are no certainties in life, but I am sure that I will always love you, Pablo Castillo,' Isabel said as she took his hand and led him to bed.

The death of Isabel's mother had an impact on Pablo that was unforeseen. In the months that followed her death, there was no recurrence of the depression which had been repeated at regular intervals ever since his exile had begun. Instead, there was now a growing dislocation from his homeland that he could never have envisaged. It extinguished the intense longing to return to the country he had always loved and fermented his loathing for the military regime which he found more and more difficult to separate from the country itself.

Although he knew that there were many people in Chile who still felt like he did about social injustice, there was no doubt in his mind now that there were many in his country who would condone what had happened to Isabel's mother. He kept returning to what he now accepted as the truth – that persecution and injustice were widespread in his homeland. He was no longer sure if or when he would ever want to return to Chile. What he had no doubt about was that he wanted never to be parted from Isabel. She was the only sure element in his future and where they were to live out that future now seemed of little consequence.

Manuel had phoned Pablo to suggest that they meet up for a drink given the news of the death of Isabel's mother. Besides, Manuel wanted to seek advice from Pablo on the mental health of a friend who was causing him concern.

'Do you think that DINA killed Isabel's mother?' Manuel asked.

'The official account is that she had a heart attack, which they deny any responsibility for. The family believe it was a conspiracy, although Isabel prefers not to speculate about how she died. I can't get out of my mind that the last thing her mother said was that she knew they would come for her.'

'Since before I fled Chile, I heard stories even prior to the coup about how the military and the police conspired to infiltrate left-wing parties and trade unions. Those stories made a few of us wonder who we could trust and led to speculation about who among all our friends and acquaintances might have been betrayers.'

'Really? Did you or your friends identify any?'

Manuel confirmed that he and his friends had their suspicions and often those focused on one or two colleagues they had never heard of again after the coup. However, one had to be careful about what remains conjecture as they may have been murdered and disappeared, for being honourable to the cause. However, there was the possibility that the authorities may have rescued and hidden their spies to prevent them suffering the recrimination that would have followed a betrayal being exposed.

'I knew there was foreign interference, but I never thought that there was local infiltration of those political organisations that supported the Allende Government,' Pablo said.

'It's impossible to gauge the scale of it but there is good evidence to believe that it was not uncommon.'

'Why do you and others think that?'

'From the accounts of the interrogations that we have heard from those who were arrested and tortured, but who managed to survive. Many were surprised at the knowledge the interrogators had of all sorts of things such as meetings, members, friendships and activities, which could only have been known by someone with inside involvement.'

'I wasn't aware of any of that. I must be naïve. What you have told me contaminates so much of what I have held onto – the pristine honour of our people.'

'I don't think you should be so hard on yourself for not realising there were spies among us. And anyway, we are still talking about no more than a handful of people. The vast majority of colleagues, be they in exile or still living in Chile, remain loyal to the same things we believe in.'

'It makes me wonder whether I can trust all the Chileans I know, even those who have ended up in exile here.'

'Surely everyone here can be trusted. Why would an infiltrator go through all the privations of life as a refugee, when they could be provided with a much better life back in Chile by their protectors?'

'Possibly because they are being paid vast sums of money to do just that. But yes, you're probably right about fellow refugees. However, for those people of our persuasion still living in Chile, how can they be sure who to trust among their friends and acquaintances?'

'The simple answer is they can't. That's why I think it's better to be in exile than in Chile, at least for the duration of the dictatorship. At what point afterwards, if at all, will the truth be revealed about all the plotting, torture and killing that came with the coup?'

'It creates doubts about whether I would ever want to move back to Chile, whatever comes after the fall of the military government.'

'We're no different to anybody else. There are no certainties in this world. You have to live the best you can in the present and take all the good you are able to from that, come what may. I'm trying to remind myself of that these days.'

'What about the other matter you mentioned that you wanted to talk to me about?'

'Oh yes, Jorge Costas! Do you know him?'

'I think I met him at a party of yours. He didn't stay long as he had an argument with a couple of people who were trying to placate him about something he was angry about. I have never seen him at any other event, so I don't know anything about him other than that.'

'There's a lot to tell.'

Chapter 8

Manuel had known Jorge in Chile, in the main through the party, but also including the brief period when they had been held in detention in the national football stadium in Santiago. Jorge was from Antofagasta, the major port city for copper and nitrate exports in the north of the country. He had been a leading trade union figure and had been taken into custody while in Santiago and tortured in the weeks following the coup. In his career as a national trade union leader, he had built contacts with trade unions in other parts of the world, and it was a British trade union that had successfully campaigned for his release to the UK. He had arrived in Bristol to much excitement among the Chilean refugee community. It was not long after that Manuel realised that Jorge was not the person he had known and admired in Chile.

From the start in Bristol, Jorge had found it difficult to settle into a life that was so different from what he had been used to in Chile. His English was poor and had remained so, which was not only an obstacle to developing friendships with anyone other than those who could speak Castellano, but also became an impediment to taking up and holding down any training and employment opportunities. With assistance from the trade union that had sponsored his release from Chile, he had taken up labouring jobs, but he had been sacked several times for either poor attendance or aggressive behaviour. Manuel had learned from Jorge that he had suffered prolonged and brutal torture, including mock executions, electric shocks, and waterboarding while in captivity.

While Jorge could be warm and communicative at times, he drank too much and often became aggressive and threatening, for no apparent reason. After a year in exile, there was no further assistance for Jorge from the British trade union and signs of more serious problems surfaced once he became long-term unemployed. He lived on social security benefits, but often ran out of money well before the day he received his benefits payment, resulting in him demanding money from other refugees, and sometimes from people in the street.

What resulted was that his friendships with most other Chilean refugees in the city became strained, although Manuel and a couple of others remained loyal and took on what became a duty to help him, including socialising with him at the weekend. It was not long before Manuel became aware that in addition to the heavy consumption of alcohol, Jorge was taking amphetamines which made him hyperactive for periods, followed by times when he was depressed and withdrawn. Manuel was not sure if there were other drugs that he was taking. His concerns had come to a head after being called to the city centre police station in the early hours of a Sunday morning.

Jorge had been arrested for an attempted break-in of a pharmacy, although he had not gained access and the police found no evidence of anything having been stolen. Jorge had refused to communicate with the police, but he had written down Manuel's name and phone number on a notepad. After Manuel's intervention, the police let him go with a caution and Manuel had taken him home to find the place in a dreadful state of neglect. Manuel and a couple of friends had returned there the next day and spent several hours cleaning it and washing the dirty clothing that had been discarded on the floor throughout the flat. Jorge had refused to take part in the clean-up and stayed in bed for the duration of it. Following that episode, Manuel became convinced that Jorge's mental health was in a precarious state and had decided to seek advice from Pablo.

'You need to remember that I am a psychiatric nursing assistant and hardly qualified to diagnose mental health. If indeed it is a mental-health problem that Jorge has,' replied Pablo, after listening without interruption to all that Manuel had to tell him about Jorge.

'There's definitely something wrong and it's getting worse. Drugs and alcohol abuse might be a factor, but they are not the primary cause. His behaviour has become strange and erratic, even when he does not appear to be drinking or doing drugs. He needs to see a doctor, but he just shakes his head when I suggest that. There must be something that can be done.'

'Only if he agrees to see a doctor and accepts a course of treatment. If he doesn't then all you can do is make him aware that there are services that can help him and encourage him to use them.'

Pablo offered to go with Manuel to talk to him about how he could get help, but he emphasised that no one could be forced into treatment, unless of course they do something that is really harmful to themself or to others. If that were to happen, the person could be sectioned under mental health legislation and held for treatment in a secure ward in a psychiatric hospital.

'I'd appreciate it if you could come with me to talk to him, Pablo. Maybe he will take advice from you because you work in mental health.'

It took many attempts before they managed to meet with Jorge. On several occasions they went to his flat, varying the days and times of the day of each visit, but he never opened the door. Manuel knew that he was inside on most of those occasions. It was only when they called at the flat early one Sunday morning that Jorge at last opened the door. On entering the flat, both Manuel and Pablo were taken aback by what they encountered.

There was barely space to make one's way down the hallway, with so much junk and old newspapers, often stacked up to the ceiling, in untidy piles in every room, leaving little room to move around. Pablo noticed that there were women's and men's clothing and was surprised that they had been kept in separate piles, which made him smile as it was the only indication of order within all the chaos. It was the same in the living room where there was nowhere to sit without moving piles of stuff from the sofa and chairs. When Jorge did not respond to Manuel's question asking if it was okay to move them, Manuel did so anyway.

'Where do you get all this stuff from, Jorge?'

'I have kept everything that people have given me. I also go round skips. Do you think I've stolen all this?' asked Jorge, as his tone of voice changed to one of irritation.

'No. I just wondered why you need to collect so much stuff.'

'It can come in useful. You never know what will happen in the future.'

'I asked Pablo to come round to tell you how you can get help with your health problems. Do you remember Pablo? You met him at a party of mine last year.'

'Don't remember him! What health problems?'

'You know things haven't been going well for a while, Jorge. Some of us are worried about how you are coping. You can get help you know. We all need help from time to time.'

'They haven't told me I have health problems.'

'Good to see you again, Jorge. How have you been?' Pablo asked.

'Who are you?'

'I'm Pablo, a friend of Manuel. I met you briefly at a party last year, but it was only a short encounter so I can see why you wouldn't remember.'

'I don't want to remember those things they keep telling me of.'

'Who keeps on telling you things? Your friends?'

'No, they're not friends. I don't like them. I wish they'd leave me alone.'

'Do they talk to you a lot then?'

'Yes, and I don't like it. I tell them to leave me alone, but they keep coming back.'

'You can get help to get rid of the voices? Is that right, you have voices speaking to you?'

'Do they talk to you too?'

'No, but I have known others who they talk to. They got help so they don't hear the voices anymore. You can get help too. How about seeing a doctor? With treatment, you will be rid of those voices, Jorge.'

'Is it these clothes you want? I've got so many.'

'How about we make an appointment with the doctor? We will go with you if that helps.'

'I'm not going to see a doctor. He'll send me to that prison we were in together, Manuel. Remember what happened to us there.'

'No, Jorge, that was back in Chile, a long time ago. We are suggesting we go with you to see your doctor, here in Bristol.'

'You must remember what they did to us there. I can't take any more of that electric shock torture, or my head being held under filthy water until I almost drowned. I am not going back there, Manuel, and nor should you. You haven't forgotten, have you?'

'Jorge, you're getting confused. We live in England. I wouldn't ever do anything to harm you. We're just talking about you going to see your doctor to make you feel better.'

'Okay.'

'We'll call back when we've arranged an appointment. Is there anything you need now? Have you got any food to eat?'

'Lots! Do you want some?'

'No thanks, Jorge. We'll call again later in the week.'

'I'd give you some of these clothes, but they won't let me.'

'Who won't let you, Jorge?' Pablo asked.

'*They* won't. Can't you hear them?'

After they left Jorge's flat, Pablo raised Jorge's memory of when he and Manuel had been held in detention together.

'I didn't know he was tortured like that.'

'We only saw each other for a brief period when held in detention. Jorge never wanted to talk much about it and all he said to me was that he was tortured for weeks including several mock executions. Last year when I asked if memories of torture were troubling him, he insisted that he had put it all out of his mind.'

'Poor Jorge. The torture may well be at the root of his mental-health problems. There may also be some history of mental-health problems in his family, which could be a contributory factor. But that's not what's important. He does need treatment, that's for sure,' Pablo stated.

Jorge didn't answer the door when they called to take him to the appointment with his GP. Manuel and Pablo tried several more times and although he opened the door on one occasion, he neither let them in nor agreed to go with them to the surgery. Manuel then managed to convince the GP to call on

Jorge at home and although he and Pablo accompanied him on the visit, Jorge would not open the door, although they could hear that he was inside. The GP left after stating that there was nothing he could do until Jorge agreed to see him, but he told them he would see Jorge without a pre-arranged appointment, if they managed to persuade him to come to the surgery.

'This can't go on. He's sick and it's getting worse. Is there anything else we can do?' Manuel asked.

'There's nothing more to be done at this stage. It will probably get worse and that may bring about a crisis. All you can do is what you are doing – calling in to see him on a regular basis and trying to persuade him to get treatment. It won't go on like this forever.'

'I fear for what comes next. Those voices in his head leave him in a distressed state. I can see that he has been crying on those occasions when he has opened the door.'

Several weeks later, the crisis unfolded. Manuel received a telephone call after returning home from work. It was a nurse from the hospital where Pablo worked. Jorge had been admitted to hospital the previous day having been sectioned under the Mental Health Act. The police had been called by a neighbour because of a disturbance in Jorge's flat. The neighbours had thought that a fight was going on as they could hear Jorge shouting and screaming at someone who they thought must be in the flat with him. There was also banging on the walls and the sound of plates being smashed.

By the time the police arrived, the only noise was Jorge crying and begging the voices in his head to leave him alone. The police made a forced entry to find Jorge cowering in the corner, crying and shaking. Nobody else was in the flat. The place was in a chaotic state. The police called a doctor and Jorge had been taken to the psychiatric hospital. Jorge's GP surgery had given the hospital Manuel's contact details, as he was listed in their records as his next of kin, unbeknown to Manuel.

'Could you come up to the hospital not only to see Jorge, but it would be helpful for us to know more about him from you, in addition to what we have found out from his GP?' the nurse said.

'Of course. How is he?'

'He's sedated now but he has been through a terrible ordeal. It's best that he rests tomorrow, so perhaps you could come to see him the day after. After you see him we can have a talk and you can fill us in on what you know of him. Does he speak English? He hasn't said much, but what he has said is in Spanish, we think.'

'Yes he understands a bit of English. He's speaking his native language, Castellano. When I come to see Jorge, I'd like to bring someone else he knows. Is that okay? He's a colleague of yours who also works in the hospital, although you may not know him. His name is Pablo Castillo.'

'Yes I know him, though not well. See you at four on Thursday. And feel free to bring Pablo along.'

Their first visit to see Jorge did not last long. It was as if Jorge did not know either of them. He did not communicate, spending most of the time staring into the distance and not appearing to have heard anything that was said to him, even though they spoke in Castellano with him and then in English to see if that made any difference. Towards the end of the visit, Jorge turned to smile at Manuel, after he had told him he would visit a couple of times a week until he got better and was able to return home.

Pablo promised to pop in a few times a week to see him, but Jorge did not respond, which Pablo thought could be because he was wearing a nurse's uniform. Manuel and Pablo visited regularly over the next few months, but nothing changed, with Jorge showing no sign of stress or trauma, yet saying nothing in response to what they said to him. They tried asking him about the past in Chile, as well as keeping Jorge informed of what was happening within the Chilean refugee community, not only in Bristol, but in other parts of the country. They took him for walks outside in the hospital gardens, or to the hospital canteen to see if getting him out of the ward would have a positive effect. But nothing made any difference.

Jorge gave the impression that he had no past that he could remember and showed no interest in the present, or in his future. Manuel was having increasing difficulty with the regular visiting regime. None of the discussions with medical staff made much sense and he wondered how long he could put himself through the ordeal of expectancy before every visit and then depression after it ended. He needed to talk to Pablo.

'It's not as if there has been any improvement since he was brought into hospital. That's months ago now! If he can remember anything, he has lost all interest in it, whether it be in the distant or recent past. I don't know if he even wants to go home now. Everything is met with a silent gaze ahead. I just feel sad and empty after every visit,' Manuel explained.

Pablo replied that he had spoken to staff on the ward and found out that on occasions Jorge talked with other patients and showed empathy and concern, especially to those going through a bad time or getting frustrated. However, he hadn't responded to any therapy sessions, though Jorge had told the Charge Nurse that he would be interested in what was called Industrial Therapy, which consisted of going to work at the hospital workshops during the week. That was due to start the following week.

'That may prompt some improvement. It also means that we can cut out the weekday visits and go to see him at the weekend,' added Pablo.

'I didn't know that he spoke with others. Do you think that indicates that he does not want to have anything to do with his past and those who share that with him?'

'Perhaps. You should ask for a meeting with the psychiatrist and ask him what he thinks and for his prognosis of Jorge.'

'I will do. It sounds positive about the work therapy, but I can't see how he will manage to keep to a work routine. I'll happily reduce my visits to once a week, which is much more manageable for me and less distressing to be honest.'

'As to a return to how he was before he had his mental-health problems, that's rare. The drugs may prevent a further crisis, but they often leave the patient without any drive and with only limited concentration. Perhaps, they will develop better drugs in the not-too-distant future.'

'Pablo, do you think he will ever talk about the torture and abuse he suffered during his detention after the coup? I don't mean with us, but in any therapy session. That could help him perhaps.'

'You should talk to the psychiatrist about all that. I'm no expert, but my understanding is that the longer he goes without any improvement, the less likely he is to return to normal function with respect to either memories of the past or engagement with the present.'

By the following year, Manuel had settled into a pattern of visiting Jorge in hospital once a month. Jorge had not managed to attend the industrial therapy beyond the first day. The reduction in Jorge's drug dosage, which was intended to maintain his drive to attend and also boost his concentration levels, resulted in a deterioration, with him again hearing voices and his distress returning. After the drug dosage had been increased to eradicate these psychotic episodes, Jorge was unable to keep to the discipline required by the work programme.

Manuel found little cause for optimism from his discussions with the psychiatrist and concluded that he was more intent on reducing Manuel's expectations of an improvement in Jorge's mental health. On more than one occasion he advised

Manuel that the only chance of effective therapy and care was dependent on the development of better drugs. When Manuel told Pablo this, he remarked that the trialling of drugs was the most demanding thing he had to deal with in his work, because most of the drug trials lacked refinement and left patients in a permanent state of confusion and often suffering incontinence.

Manuel had taken a long detour home over the Clifton Downs after that talk with Pablo. It was dark and he encountered no one as he made his way to what he considered his place of hidden solitude within the city. From time to time, he caught glimpses of a bank of lights from the distant conurbation and he heard the steady drone of traffic, but tonight he felt no connection to anything other than what was in his mind. Stopping at a bench facing a wooded area with a view of nothing but darkness, the dam he had built over the last year, broke. He wept for Jorge and for every one of his fellow Chileans who had been subjected to torture causing irrecoverable damage to their life and to the lives of those close to them. A wave of grief swept Manuel away, drowning any optimism he had for justice ever being realised in this world.

For some time after, he sat still and silent, until the rain soaked through his clothes to his skin and stirred him again. He began to shout a frenzy of curses into the endless darkness, calling out all the brutality and injustice. There was no hope of ever seeing Jorge restored to health and, despite what Pablo had said about a possible combination of factors being responsible for how Jorge had ended up, Manuel would never change his view that this was a crime done by others, and he would hold them responsible for it. If he were ever to have the opportunity to exact revenge for this and the killings of his other friends in Chile, he vowed that he would surely take it.

Chapter 9

In 1979, over three years after the death of Isabel's mother, Pablo qualified as a Psychiatric nurse. He celebrated at a city centre pub with colleagues most of whom were now also friends. They outnumbered the Chilean friends he had invited, which reflected the changes in his life over the last few years. He had stopped attending party meetings which was the way he kept in regular touch with compatriots, but he continued to meet with Manuel on a frequent basis. Other than that, the only other Chileans he had regular contact with were Carmen and Dolores when Isabel invited them round to their flat, which happened on a frequent basis. Every month without fail he wrote to his father in Chile. He always replied within the month. Twice a year he wrote to his two brothers though it was only at Christmas that he got a response from one or other of them.

He had become a trade union representative at the hospital and played an active role and often socialised with fellow representatives and work colleagues who had become friends. Every weekend he played squash at a local club and had made friends there. All of these new friends were at the celebration. It was an early autumn evening when he walked home with Isabel and for the first time in ages he began to think of the past, back to the time shortly after the death of Isabel's mother which had changed everything.

'Do you remember my paranoid state when I was obsessed with those times preceding the coup and up to that time that we fled for our lives? I couldn't understand how I had been so unaware of infiltration in the party. I put it down to either a flawed memory or my warped judgement of people. I lost all confidence in myself.'

'I remember you being adamant that you would never again accept anything you were told by anybody without applying a lot of scrutiny. You aren't paranoid like that now, are you?'

'No. Nowadays those times seldom come to mind. I'm surprised now when being Chilean comes up in a conversation. How about going to the Italian restaurant round the corner to continue the celebrations? It's still early.'

'Why not. It's not every day we celebrate you gaining professional qualifications. I never thought you would ever accept the hospital's offer of training.'

After the first glass of wine, Pablo took Isabel's hand.

'There's another matter for us to discuss. It's not anything bad, so no need to look concerned. The last time we talked about getting married, we left it that we would do it when we returned to Chile. I have always loved you. Will you marry me?'

'You mean that I don't have to wait indefinitely for us to get back to Chile? If that's the case, I will say yes.'

'Great! I'm embarrassed that I made it conditional on us returning to Chile. But there's more! I always wanted us to have children, but what has changed is my wish not to delay it until a return to Chile. When do you think we could try to start a family?'

'Hold on. You've only just asked me to marry you.'

'I'm not expecting you to agree to start a family right away. I just want to make it clear that there is no need for the delay I had imposed. Of course, it is for you to decide when you want to have a child.'

'I want to continue to work for a couple of years now that I have been made a team manager, which means the earliest I could safely come off the pill is in about eighteen months' time. I will want to go back to work after having a child. It's not for me to be a stay-at-home mother.'

'I wouldn't want you to be anything other than what you are.'

'Let's drink to lovers the world over!' Isabel proposed as she took a sip of wine and leaned over to give Pablo a long lingering kiss.

'It's right to focus on the opportunities that we are lucky to have been given. It's ironic that after my mother's killing I've spent so much of that time locked into memories of the past, whereas you have distanced yourself from the past.'

'Yes, we have changed. Nobody knows what lies ahead and for how long one will be on this earth. We shouldn't waste time trying to live in a past that is dead and gone.'

'The time I spent thinking back to past times is all done for me too. I have a life of my own to live, which is how my mother would have wanted me to be. It's good that we have found a way forward together. Here's to enjoying the best moments in life, before they pass us by.'

The wedding took place in 1981, four months before the expected arrival of their first child. They wanted their wedding to be a special occasion for the entire Chilean community in the city. With that in mind, they spent a lot of time saving for what would be an expensive undertaking, with the intention of making it an event that would be as close as possible to a traditional Chilean wedding. Isabel had asked her sister to be her bridesmaid, but she had responded that although she would love to accept, she did not want to take the risk of leaving Chile, only to be refused re-entry on her return. That possibility she considered a very real one, due to her and her family's political activities in opposition to the dictatorship, which as ever, the regime was intent on ridding the country of.

As a consequence, Isabel asked Carmen to be her bridesmaid but only after explaining to Dolores and Jane that she could have chosen any one of them, given she held all three equally as her best friends, but she thought choosing Carmen would boost her confidence. Pablo had little trouble deciding that Manuel would be his best man, as he had long been his closest friend in Bristol. He would have loved his widowed father and his brothers to be at the wedding, but that was impractical because of his father's frail health and his brothers' unending struggle to make a living, let alone afford expensive airfares.

Pablo and Isabel never considered a church wedding. While Isabel had been baptised Catholic, she had never been brought up to attend church on a regular basis and had abandoned the last vestiges of her religion when she started university. Pablo had been a practising Catholic up to his transformation of outlook a few years earlier, when he'd come to a firm conclusion that there was no god to believe in. For both of them, the wedding reception rather than the ceremony was the important event. They decided that it would be held in a community centre to which Isabel had access through work. It had a well-equipped kitchen and Carmen and Dolores took the responsibility for the catering and drew up a menu of traditional Chilean food.

'That's the sort of authentic, Chilean food that I am sure will go down well with everyone who has been invited. We will need help to serve and clear up, but Pablo has assured me that he will organise all that. I've never actually been to a Chilean wedding. Have either of you?' asked Isabel.

'I went to one as a child but can't remember a lot about it, other than never having seen so many beautiful flowers before,' replied Dolores.

'I remember my cousin's wedding. Her parents were well-off and had aspirations to be seen as a sophisticated family with Western tastes, so they engaged a French chef to do the food. I found the food too rich for my liking and looking around the tables, so did lots of others,' added Carmen.

'They probably thought of you as some common peasant,' said Isabel.

'There are a lot of rich people in Chile who lack nothing except taste for not only Chilean food but also culture. A lot of them deny that Chile has Indigenous peoples and know nothing of their cultures. There is no Indigenous art on display in their homes and you would never find them dancing the Cueca,' added Carmen.

'I remember them well with their lives dominated by fear and hatred of anybody different from their miserable selves. I'd never accept an offer of a dance from any of them,' Dolores managed to say before her laughter could not be contained any longer.

'Well, I'm glad that none of those types will be at our wedding. We have managed to get a Chilean band that tours in many European countries. So, the Chileans will feel more at home here in Bristol than they would have at that wedding that Carmen had to endure,' explained Isabel.

At dusk, after the speeches, Manuel stood on the terrace outside with a cigarette in his hand, recalling the last wedding he had attended, in Santiago, not long before the coup occurred. On a sweltering afternoon, his ex-wife had been standing on a balcony looking out to the horizon where the snow-capped Andes towered up into the blue sky. He remembered how attractive his wife looked that day, but that image was accompanied with a haunting sense of being worried about something. He couldn't make up his mind what that was; perhaps it had been a foreboding of what was to come on the political front, or later when his marriage broke up. He considered that he was good at sensing imminent danger, much better than any of his friends past or present had ever been, but not very good at then avoiding it.

After a few moments, he wondered whether those distant memories of the wedding and those haunting concerns were a figment of his imagination. There was nothing to confirm that he could have known there would be an imminent coup, or that his relationship with his wife would deteriorate and end less than two years later. He sighed at not only how his marriage had broken up, but also how he had lost all contact with his former wife.

He turned to go back into the wedding reception where the band was tuning up when he heard raised voices at the far end of the terrace. He caught a glimpse of a man he did not recognise, who disappeared back into the hall, but it was just possible in the fading light to make out a silhouette of a woman holding a handkerchief to her eyes, with her head bowed. Manuel made his way towards her.

'Are you okay? Is there anything I can do to help?'

'No, thank you. I'm fine. I will be in a minute.'

'Oh, it's you, Carmen. Perhaps I can get you a drink? Anything else I can do?'

'That's kind of you. Yes, I would like a glass of water, please. I need a moment to get myself together before going back in.'

Manuel returned with a glass of water and a few paper napkins, which he thought may be of use to her.

'Thanks, Manuel. I know a lot about you, from Isabel and Pablo.'

'It's a pleasure to speak to you. I have known you from a distance. I know this is hardly the time to be saying this, but I have nothing other than admiration for how you have made a life for yourself after the horrors you endured.'

'Ah, you know that about me, then. I could do with a short walk before I go back in as I don't want anyone to see me in this state. Would you mind coming with me as it's getting dark? I don't feel safe walking on my own.'

'Certainly. I could do with a break from the celebrations myself. Too much enjoyment for a miserable sod like me.'

She smiled as they walked off together. After a few minutes strolling together, Manuel put his arm around her shoulder. She responded by putting her arm round his hips. They continued walking along the path towards a wooded area, without saying anything to each other.

'We should get back before we are missed,' said Carmen.

'If you'd prefer to go home rather than back into the celebrations, I can arrange for a taxi for you. I am happy to explain to Pablo and Isabel that you felt ill and needed to go home, while assuring them that there is nothing for them to worry about.'

'That's thoughtful of you, but I'm fine now apart from being a little saddened by the behaviour of someone here. Regardless, I'm not going to let that spoil this celebration for me or for anyone else.'

'If that's the case then yes, let's go back, but if you change your mind just let me know. And if you have any more trouble, I'll protect you.'

'Thanks, Manuel. I can look after myself.'

'Thank you for the walk, I enjoyed it. I'm going to stay out here and have another cigarette. I'll come in after that.'

Carmen strolled into the room just as the guitars struck up the well-known chords, and Isabel and Pablo were walking hand in hand onto the dance floor. They faced each other, smiling, she held her white handkerchief aloft, while his was held over his shoulder. A flurry of clapping and vigorous guitar strumming erupted. He strutted and danced with unrelenting energy as she glided and fluttered in response to his movements towards her. The band built up the music in speed and volume reaching a crescendo while all around clapped their hands to the rhythm. With a grand flourish the couple brought the dance to an end with Pablo placing one knee on the floor while Isabel delicately rested her foot on his raised knee.

Carmen joined in the cascade of applause as the wedding couple walked off the dance floor arm in arm. She was going to enjoy the rest of the evening, come what may. Sensing someone close behind her, she turned around to see Manuel standing looking into the distance with tears trickling down his cheeks. She took his hand and kissed him, which made her smile at her spontaneous and bold reaction to someone she barely knew. Holding her hand like he never wanted to let go, Manuel gazed down at her and smiled, but with melancholy in his eyes.

'Let's dance the Cueca and step back in time,' Carmen whispered in his ear.

They joined the other couples on the dance floor as the band started up the dance music again. There was no hesitation. It was as if they had been dancing together all their lives. They continued dancing with the occasional break for the duration of the band's performance. At the end of the evening, Manuel asked Carmen if they could continue by going to either his home or hers. Carmen nodded and gave him her address. She insisted that that they go there separately and that he should follow no less than ten minutes after she had left. He replied that he had agreed to help with the clearing up so it would be about an hour before he would get there. She told him she would wait up.

In the dark, he searched for a doorbell but could not find one, so he knocked gently on the door. Had she gone to bed or should he knock louder? He could not decide so shaking his head he turned to go home, just as the door opened. She smiled and indicated to him to come in. He kissed her briefly as he walked past and went through the open door of the living room to be met with the scent from two vases overflowing with flowers in full bloom.

'What beautiful flowers full of summer scent,' he said.

'Isabel insisted that I have them as there were more than enough flowers for her and Pablo to take home. Of course, Dolores took most of them.'

'She probably grew them in her garden.'

'Manuel, I know this a bit forward and presumptuous, but I don't want you to stay overnight. I don't want to have sex. I just thought it best to say that up front to prevent any misunderstanding.'

'Of course! I wouldn't want to do anything to upset you, but I have to tell you that you were the most beautiful woman at the wedding.'

'Thank you. I was sure you would understand about sex. Do you want anything to drink?'

'A coffee would be good. I've drunk enough alcohol for one day or perhaps several.'

'Thank you for being so kind and attentive to me. I should tell you what I was upset about at the wedding.'

'You don't need to give me an explanation.'

Carmen recounted how she had got upset with Javi because he suggested they get together later at her place. She couldn't believe him saying that given their history and that he was at the wedding with his girlfriend, Rachel. When he suggested that Carmen still fancied him, she got angry and told him that he was arrogant and that she certainly did not have any feelings for him.

'He didn't take it well and stormed off. It threw me a little, but thanks to you being so considerate, I forgot about it and had a great time after that. What made you cry when Isabel and Pablo were dancing the Cueca?'

'It was an evening of high emotion for me. We could have been altogether at a wedding in Chile. It felt like we were… that we had somehow been able to revisit with no memory of the tarnished past. Then, the thought of those who have gone and all those whose lives are now blighted, brought me back to the present.'

'You are unusual. You're a very sensitive man.'

'Well, thank you, but I should point out you hardly know me. For all you know, I could be a charming, but deceitful person.'

'I don't think so, but if you are, I will find out quickly.'

'Warning heeded! I'm glad that incident with Javi didn't stop you having a good time. Did today feel like being back in Chile for you?'

'No, but I did feel that I was among good friends, the people who mean so much to me. And yes, the music and dancing did arouse good feelings of the past. I felt proud to be Chilean for the first time in a long while.'

'I know you have been through terrible times. How have you managed to come through all of that and build a new life?'

'Well, if you are in no hurry, I'll tell you.'

Carmen explained that in the early stages of exile the problem wasn't horrendous memories but the state of denial she was locked into. She went on to talk with gratitude and affection of all the people who had helped her to make a life beyond all the trauma. She cited Dolores, Jane, Isabel, Pablo, and her therapist who had so skilfully and patiently assisted her find a way to move on to where she was now. As far as Carmen was concerned, she would forever be in debt to those people.

'And where are you now, Carmen, if I may ask?'

'Well, I am telling you, a man, about what happened to me and how I got through it. Tonight's episode with Javi shows how things have changed – I know now how to deal with upset and anxiety. Besides, I have a good job working with kids. I live independently and feel at home in a country that I knew little about, when I arrived in such a mess.'

'Don't you hold any of that anger and resentment that can eat away at one?'

'No. I've managed to avoid that. Do you?'

'I do. I sometimes get into a rage about what has happened in Chile. Not so much for myself but for the killing and torture of others. I got off lightly, though I can still get nightmares about it.'

Carmen leaned over and kissed Manuel and he reciprocated, containing his urge to go further.

'Let's say good night, Manuel. I'd like to meet up again and want to hear more of your story. How about next weekend?'

'I'd love to. Though I should warn you in advance, I have no achievements to tell you that are as impressive as yours.'

'That's for me to decide and I already like and admire the little I know.'

Chapter 10

Manuel spent a lot of the following week in a state of anticipation, but also concerned that Carmen might end up being disappointed in him. His failed marriage, as he saw it, had left him with doubts about being able to maintain a relationship and he wondered what he could offer someone as attractive as Carmen. He couldn't deny his periods of hopelessness that he was unable to break out of and he worried that would be something which would put her off getting into a relationship with him. Or worse, he worried that if they did get together, after a brief period of time it would lead to yet another relationship breaking down.

Manuel was a little older than the other Chileans he had got to know in Bristol. Often he was seen as the provider of wise counsel within the Chilean exile community. He was not sure he liked that, as it suggested to him he had less vitality and spontaneity than he wanted to possess. That would surely not be something that someone as young and attractive as Carmen would find appealing. Despite the doubts which he was unable to set aside, he could not contain his attraction to her that grew by the day in the week leading up to their first date.

On the Wednesday before the weekend they had agreed to meet, Manuel was browsing in an art shop and chose a card of a still life print of colourful flowers by Cezanne which he thought she might like. He sent that to her suggesting they meet for a stroll at a specific bench on the Downs, providing a sketch of its location on the back of the card. He also mentioned a nearby Italian restaurant that he liked, which did an excellent value lunch well into the afternoon. He wrote down his telephone number, asking her to contact him if any of these suggestions were not to her liking.

No phone call had been received so he set off early afternoon on Saturday, intent on arriving at the bench at least fifteen minutes before the time he had stated on the card. After sitting on the bench for five minutes he began worrying that his directions had not been clear. Fifteen minutes later he was convinced that indeed was the case and he got up to leave only to see Carmen strolling down the pathway towards him. He felt foolish and awkward for a moment and remained standing to greet her.

'Sorry I'm late, Manuel. I missed the bus I intended to get, and it was a while before the next one came. I'm not normally late,' she added, as they kissed.

'I was beginning to think that my directions were poor. You look beautiful in that dress.'

'Thank you. Is this a significant place for you?'

'Yes. I stopped at this bench the first time I discovered this beautiful, haven of nature within the noisy city. The Downs are not just somewhere I come to when I am struggling, but also when I am feeling good. I have been here so many times, in all seasons and in all states of mind. So much so that I think of this place as my second home in the city.'

'I feel honoured to be admitted. I have also grown to love it here, ever since Dolores introduced me to this place. She convinced me to join her on her walks on the Downs, telling me about the plants and wildflowers. Those were crucial times in my recovery. Tell me about some of your most memorable times spent on this bench.'

'I promise I will, but I should first tell you a bit about myself and my background. Shall we go for a stroll to the places I like and you can take me to those places that are special for you? Let's go first to your favourite places while I tell you a little of who I am, or who I think I am.'

They wandered off holding hands, with Carmen leading the way while Manuel started on a potted history of his childhood and youth. He had been born and brought up in Valparaiso, the major port on the Pacific coast, before the family moved to Santiago in his late teenage years. He pointed out with pride that Valparaiso was where Chile's most famous poet, Pablo Neruda, lived, before moving to a house by the shoreline about thirty miles south of the city where he lived for many years until he died, only months after the coup occurred. Manuel outlined his family and youth. He had a sister and their parents were wealthier than most, resulting in his childhood being carefree and comfortable in the main. He began to write poetry in his teenage years, but it was not until his late twenties that he had a collection published. He had written little poetry since then and had published nothing after that first collection.

By the time he went to university in Santiago, a growing chasm had emerged between him and his father, whose reactionary views clashed with his strengthening left-wing sympathies, although he explained that his father had not always been a reactionary but grew into that state of mind after a strike by his employees in his small factory that produced mahogany furniture. His mother was forever caught between them, but she had never allowed her love for her son to be diminished.

Following the coup, which had a devastating effect on him, not least because he had failed to foresee it, Manuel was held in prison and tortured until a Member of Parliament for a Bristol constituency managed to get the UK Government to successfully press the Chilean authorities to release him into exile. He and his wife were the first Chilean refugees to arrive in Bristol and they had enjoyed some publicity in the local press due, in no small measure to the MP describing them as accomplished poets. His wife also wrote poetry, was more productive, and in his view, much better at it than he was.

The publicity had opened doors in terms of getting work and earning a decent living in Bristol. He secured a part-time post at the university lecturing on Latin-American literature and supplemented his income with private work, teaching Spanish. After a brief period, the marriage ended, which Manuel put down to them simply growing apart. His wife moved to London and contact ended between them.

'A poet then. Do you still write poetry?' Carmen asked.

'Seldom, not since I was young and carefree.'

'I'd be interested in reading your collection. Is it for sale here?'

'No, it was published in Chile, but I have a copy. Please don't feel obliged to say you like it if you don't. I'm spending my time these days trying to write a novel, and it's beginning to take shape though I'm not sure of the full story, and don't yet know how it ends.'

'What's it about? When do you think you will have it finished?'

Manuel stated that he was not sure yet what it was about at its core. He knew he was writing about exile using his own experiences and those of others, but the plot was not yet fully clear. He could see some themes emerging but was not sure yet what would emerge as the main one. As to when it would be finished, that was not in his hands, because he'd decided at the start that it would only be completed when his exile was over.

'That could mean it might never be finished.'

'A possibility, yes, but in my view unlikely. I can get depressed about what has happened in Chile and the death and suffering caused to good friends I knew and loved. Writing stories of exile keeps me from dwelling on the futility I can sometimes feel.'

'Pablo once described you as the sage among the refugee community here in Bristol. He thinks you have a lot of wisdom, or at least more than others do. Did you know that?'

'Well, I know there is that view, but Pablo is a good friend who I learn from as much as he might do from me. Perhaps it's because I arrived here before most Chileans which enables me to give advice to all those who arrived after I did.'

'Javi told me shortly after he met you for the first time, that he admired you more than any other man he had met here.'

'He does a lot of publicity work which I admire him for. I have less interest in political meetings these days and I reckon Javi has ambitions to play the leading role in the Forum, which is fine by me. Enough of all that! Tell me more about your love of the Downs.'

Carmen explained it was where she rediscovered the beauty of the world through her senses; something that had lain dormant behind the trauma that was suffocating her. It was as if the colours and scents of the wildflowers had reacquainted her with who she was.

'I love Dolores. She's funny and always positive. She knows a lot that only Indigenous people do. I did know of her love of the natural world and that is at the heart of why she is such a generous soul.'

'Look at those whitebeam tree flowers and those beautiful orchids, over there. And further along, there is the scent of wild thyme, which I never noticed until Dolores brought it to my attention. While all that stimulation of the senses contributed to my healing, now it's making me hungry. Shall we go and eat? It's always better to get to know a person over a good bottle of wine.'

After the waiter poured the chilled white wine, Carmen made a toast to Dolores, who she called her force of nature.

'So, more about you. Why did you and your wife split up? Sorry, that's a bit forward. You don't have to tell me if you'd rather not.'

'I'm okay with that. We had grown apart which is not that surprising given we got together when very young, in our first year at university. We found ourselves thrown together in a hugely different world after fleeing the country. For some, that can result in a stronger bond, but for us, that was not the case.'

'Why was that?'

'I have always been prone to depression. Bad episodes where I don't sleep well, though perhaps less so now than back then.'

'You both shared a talent for poetry. Sounds like you had more in common than most couples.'

'Perhaps. While a successful relationship depends on having some shared ideas or values in life, it's also important to have differences. I think relationships can fail because the partners are too similar.'

'I never thought about that before. There would have to be differences between them that somehow fit together in a positive way, or it wouldn't work.'

'Yes, that's true. And if I may ask, why did your relationship not work out with Javi?'

'I used to think that the trauma of what happened in prison was the key factor but now I think there were other reasons. I needed a lot of patient care and attention that he was unable to provide. I lost trust in him, which I think is an absolute must for a relationship to survive and thrive.'

'I agree. I hope you can trust me, Carmen. I like your take on things, but I accept that we hardly know each other, and that it takes time to build trust.'

'Given this is our first date, we are getting to know a lot about each other very quickly. But yes, I am still inclined to be wary, although I also very much like what I am getting to know of you. There's no hurry, is there?'

'Not at all. I'm happy to go at your pace. I just enjoy being in your company.'

'I also need to hear what you think of me, not only what you find physically attractive about me. For a long time, I didn't want to be attractive to any man, because all they seemed interested in was my body.'

'I love how you talk, how you express yourself and how you laugh. I like your sceptical take on memories of the past. All of those things wrapped up with how physically attractive you are is a powerful combination for me. I understand why you are wary of getting physically involved and I hope we can overcome that. I can be as patient as you need.'

'Just to reassure you, I don't think I have been permanently turned off sex. In fact, I know I haven't. Nevertheless, you will have to be patient. I have to feel right, and if and when we get to that stage, it will be a big thing for me.'

'Of course. I accept that. Let's just spend time with each other. I'd like to meet up a couple of times a week. Is that too much for you?'

'No. That sounds right.'

Carmen had invited her close friends to dinner. There was a nagging worry that accompanied the growing sense of excitement about her regular meetings with Manuel. Would she ever be able to have and sustain a sexual relationship? She enjoyed the frequent kissing with Manuel but was unsure how she would feel were they to have sex. She felt attracted to him, but she had worries that intercourse would trigger a flashback to the rapes. Carmen had not told anyone else that she and Manuel were seeing each other, but she was anxious to share her feelings and concerns with close friends she trusted.

'It all sounds good to me. Of course you would have some misgivings about sex. I can't think of anyone better for you to get together with. I've thought for years that the miserable sod could be doing with someone to cheer him up. Spends too much time being loyal and attentive to others,' Dolores said, as she filled everyone's glass.

'I couldn't agree more. He's a generous-hearted person, who deserves someone special like you. It sounds as if it is all going very well, Carmen. Anything worthwhile takes time,' Jane added.

'Yes, I enjoy his company and find him attractive. I get excited about meeting up, but I'm worried about how I will react if we get intimate. We do kiss, but it's the stage beyond that concerns me.'

'That's hardly surprising, Carmen. Just go at your own pace, but if it is such a worry why not arrange a session with Becky? I'm sure that would be helpful,' replied Jane.

'Yes, I think I will. I'm not unduly pessimistic about getting through this but during that prolonged period of trauma, I recall how I never wanted to appear attractive to a man again, let alone be touched. I have certainly moved on since that, don't you think?'

Dolores topped up their glasses and made a toast.

'You've moved on a huge distance. Here's to you and Manuel. Let us know how it goes. I do love a romance,' toasted Dolores.

Becky agreed to see Carmen soon after she had made the call. After listening to Carmen's account of how she felt and what her concerns were, she assured her that it was only to be expected that she would be concerned about having sex, but that she was positive this could be worked through. She advised Carmen to raise the matter with Manuel as it was her view that talking over her concerns with him was essential to building the trust between them which was the crucial factor in Carmen overcoming what Becky referred to as her 'last hurdle.' Although Carmen raised the worry that this may then put pressure on Manuel, which she didn't want to do, Becky convinced her that working out a shared way forward was the best way to resolve it. If he was not up to that, then at least she would know it at this early stage.

A few days after, she met up with Manuel. She had suggested it would be best she come to his flat as she thought that he might feel more comfortable being in his own home, when she raised the issue with him. When they met, she not only set out her feelings on the matter but also told Manuel that Becky had advised her to discuss everything with him. When she had finished, she sat looking at the floor, wondering whether she should have done so. He got up from his chair and sat next to her on the sofa, taking her hand in his.

'It had already occurred to me that us being intimate could well cause you some anxiety. I don't deny that I want us to make love, but only when you feel you want that. This is not something worth worrying about.'

'That's reassuring. I don't want a mechanical approach to this though. Don't check with me that I am feeling okay before you do anything. If it is too much, too soon, I will let you know. As long as you don't get offended with me if I call a halt, that's the key thing for me. I'm very fond of you, Manuel.'

'I'll never go further if you ask me to stop at any stage. You can be certain of that.'

The day after, Carmen arrived home from work, to find a

large bouquet of flowers by the door with a card on which was
written:

> *I will bring you happy flowers from the mountains,*
> *bluebells, dark hazels, and rustic baskets of kisses.*
> *I want to do with you*
> *what spring does with the cherry trees.*[1]

She picked up the flowers and took a slow, deep inhalation.
It was then that Carmen knew that they would make love when
they met up at the weekend.

Manuel sat up in bed as Carmen lay asleep beside him. Looking
down at her, he smiled, unable to recall feeling so happy and
content. He felt as carefree as he had ever been during his life
in exile. He smiled as he looked down at her lying naked and
so alluring, moving him to run his fingers through her dark,
lustrous hair spread out in an abandoned entanglement over
the pristine white pillow. She stirred from her sleep and opened
her eyes. On catching sight of him, a smile spread over her face.

'Sorry to have woken you but I could not resist caressing
your gorgeous hair.'

'I am happy for you to caress every part of me. You must
never stop doing that unless you stop loving me.'

'How could I ever stop loving you?'

'Nothing is impossible and few things last forever, as we
have both come to know.'

If they were going to be sleeping together, Manuel knew
he had to tell her about his nightmare. He recounted to her
how it had contaminated his marriage and other relationships
and admitted his fear that it might finish their relationship.

---

1   Neruda, Pablo, 'Juegas todos los dias', W.S. Merwin, (trans.), *Selected Poems*,
    Penguin, 1975.

He described it as his curse and when she asked him why he defined it in that way, he explained as best he could. The guilt was always there whether in the nightmare or when awake. Not one of his four friends had been heard of again and he had come to accept that all of them had all been brutally killed, as did their relatives and other friends. He could not bear to think about the terror they endured before their killing. Why he was released and not them was something that he still had not found an explanation for. There was no treacherous act on his part, but he somehow knew that his friends had been betrayed by somebody. Why he had survived remained a mystery to him.

Carmen asked him why he would think that she would ever lose interest in him on account of his nightmares, given what had happened to her. He nodded and then smiled.

'It's Saturday. Shouldn't you be writing the book?' Carmen asked.

'I am wondering whether to continue with it. The primary reason for embarking on it was as a way to rid myself of the nightmare or at least reduce how often it occurred. I now reckon that falling in love with you is the antidote and I don't need to continue with the writing.'

'You told me that you had come to enjoy writing the story, as you did not know how it would end. It would be a shame not to continue with it. Besides, I think you being a writer is a big part of the attraction for me, so you may have to see it through if you don't want to lose me.'

'Extortion then! If that's a condition for your love, then I have no option. If I am allowed to put conditions on our relationship, I would like us to consider moving in together, to a bigger place than either of us has at the moment. What do you think?'

'Seems a good idea. We are both in secure jobs and earning enough, so why not buy our own place. Let's go to an estate agent and arrange some viewings.'

'I was thinking more of spending the morning in bed with you.'

'We can go back to bed later on. Let's go and find our new home.'

They fell into a routine of staying in Manuel's flat during the week as it was conveniently located for both their jobs and living in Carmen's flat at the weekend. After almost a year that living arrangement ended after an offer was accepted on a three-bed flat that they both liked, and which was well situated for both of them getting to work. Contracts were due to be exchanged in the coming weeks and they were already well advanced in agreeing how it would be decorated and fitted out.

'Which room should we have for the baby?' Manuel asked.

'Oh, let's not get ahead of ourselves. I may not be able to get pregnant given the sexually transmitted disease I carried for so long after the rapes, and anyway we agreed that I wouldn't come off the pill for a couple of years yet. Are you changing your mind about that?'

'No. I'm fine with what we agreed. Just getting carried away with the excitement of setting up home with you.'

'Everything will be settled with time, but I don't want us to make assumptions about the future, as it may never happen as we want it to.'

Chapter 11

It was a sunny October morning, when the air had lost the warmth of summer and the leaves on the trees were showing the first signs of decay. Pablo knocked on the front door hoping that Manuel would not be at home. He knew that Carmen would be at work and that this was a day when Manuel worked at home, so he stood on the doorstep and awaited a response. He was at the point of turning away in relief when the door opened.

'Sorry about calling this early, Manuel, but there's something I have to tell you.'

'Come in!

'Jorge is dead.'

Manuel slumped into an easy chair by the fireplace and rocked backwards and forwards. He suddenly got up, stood at the window and stared out into the distance.

'I knew this day would come. How?' Manuel asked.

'It's not clear. He must have wandered onto the train line near the woods just beyond the hospital grounds. It may have been suicide as he was lying on the track, according to the train driver, who is in a terrible state. It happened last night, and I was phoned by a colleague early this morning.'

'It may be deemed suicide, but it never will be that for me. Poor Jorge.'

'You were a good friend to him. You did all you could.'

'Thanks, Pablo. It was not enough though, was it?'

'What else could you have done? Who is to know whether he intended suicide or not, given his state of mind. Of course, there will be an inquest and then an official verdict.'

'What do I care about an inquest and an official verdict. I know why he got sick and why he ended up as he did. I don't need anyone else to tell me. I knew him better than anyone here. He was a decent, courageous man who never deserved such an end. I will never forget him.'

'Should we have some coffee now? I'll make it if you tell me where everything is.'

'It's all on the worktop. Help yourself, Pablo. I need to go out and walk.'

'To the Downs?'

'Where else? Close the door behind you when you leave. Thank you for all you did for Jorge, I appreciate it. I'll phone you about the funeral arrangements.'

Manuel told Carmen when she returned from work but his voice tailed off before he finished all that he wanted to say.

'Oh Manuel, how sad! I know how fond of him you were.'

'No relatives and no friends around him at the end. Little wonder he lost the will to live. I feel desperately sad about his last few years when he slipped away from us, but I also feel consumed by anger at those I hold responsible.'

'I can understand how aggrieved you must feel. You need to be careful you don't get trapped in the hurt and rage you feel now.'

'It's hard to be wise at times like this. Jorge became such a forlorn man after he got ill. I'll try to focus on his commitment and courage before that happened. He achieved so much for working people.'

'What about his family? He must have some.'

Manuel explained that he had a brother and sister who he understood lived in Antofagasta. Jorge had never given Manuel an address and he never had contact with them after he got ill, according to the hospital.

'Some day one of us should track down his relatives and friends in Chile and tell them of his death and of how much he was admired for what he did in his life.'

Manuel took on the responsibility for the arrangements of Jorge's funeral. It was a simple cremation at which he alone spoke and where there were only a handful of people present. He recalled his friendship with Jorge and cited meetings and conferences they had attended together before the coup, when Jorge's speeches had been full of passion and humour. They had met up briefly when they were held in detention together after the military coup, but it wasn't until Jorge arrived in exile that they renewed contact. Manuel described the very different character he'd encountered in Bristol. It was as if Jorge had forgotten who he was. He had no wish to revisit the recent past, which had clearly scarred him.

He may have deteriorated into a man with no hope for the future, but that was not who he was. Manuel stated he would bear witness to who Jorge was at his core – a man who acted for others, with a stand-out generosity. He would never forget him and the debt so many others owed him.

'That was wonderful what you said and how you said it,' said Carmen at the wake afterwards.

'It was no less than the truth. I loved him for who he was and today at least I am setting aside the anger that his death has left me with.'

'It's not much of a turnout. I am surprised that I didn't see Javi at the crematorium and he hasn't turned up at the wake.'

Manuel informed her that Javi had approached him a few days ago and had suggested that he should speak at the funeral as he was the Secretary of the Forum for Chilean Refugees. Manuel said no to that, given how Javi had shunned Jorge before he'd ended up in hospital. Only he, Pablo and Dolores had bothered to visit Jorge for all those years in hospital.

'Javi didn't take that too well and I'm glad he didn't turn up. I have come to dislike him due to his insensitivity and arrogance.'

'That doesn't surprise me, but let's not dwell on it. There's more than enough to be sad about today.'

The night after the wake, it returned. Manuel awoke shouting out in terror.

'You're safe, Manuel. You're here with me,' Carmen said as she embraced him. His gasping for breath eased.

'I'm sorry.'

'You almost fell out of bed onto the floor. What was it?'

'The nightmare. The one I told you about. It's come back.'

'It's hardly surprising given Jorge's death.'

'I suppose so but it's been so long since I had that nightmare. I was sure it had gone for good. His death has rekindled all that terror deep within me. Surely it's not going to start up again like before.'

'Of course you are going to have dreams after losing your friend. I don't think it will persist. Things are different now. We're together and I love you.'

'Yes, you're right. I need to expect this given what has happened. Nor do I think it will return on the same basis as before. I won't let it blight my life in the way it once did.'

'I'm the living proof of moving on from trauma and grief.'

'What would I do without you?'

'If you're lucky you will never find out.'

The inquest was held two months after.

'It was an open verdict,' Manuel told Carmen when they met up after work.

'What does that mean?'

'There is a possibility of suicide, but there is no clear evidence of intent. I feel relieved and in an odd way happy for Jorge, despite having said all along that the official verdict would mean nothing to me.'

'That's a really good outcome. I'm pleased for you and for Jorge.'

'It will also be good news for his relatives and friends back in Chile when we tell them if and when we go back to Chile.'

'And when might that be? Not anytime soon from what I understand.'

Manuel explained that there was a decree introduced by the dictatorship a couple of years ago which allowed exiles to return, but only those that had not been proscribed as criminals and terrorists. He was adamant that he would never return under any circumstances, until there was a democratically elected government in place, which was intent on exposing all the torture and killing that had gone on. There would have to be some form of justice and reparation for all those crimes.

'So, you're right I won't be going back anytime soon, but the dictator's new constitution, imposed last year, requires that there to be a plebiscite in seven years' time, when there will be a choice to vote for him continuing as president or for free elections to be held to establish a democratically elected government.'

'Of course, we all know he is a man of his word,' replied Carmen.

'Well, there is that, but he'll have difficulty even with his friends in the USA and the UK if he doesn't comply with his own constitution.'

'Perhaps he'll win the vote for the dictatorship to continue.'

'In a fair and free election? I can't see that being the outcome, can you?' Manuel asked.

'I've no idea. I don't spend the time you do on trying to track what is happening there, but you often say the population there is always being fed the threat of violence and chaos were there to be a return to democracy. You never can tell the effect of that propaganda. I've got more interesting news.'

Dolores had just told Carmen that she and Jane were about to move in together and to celebrate they had invited her and Manuel over for dinner.

'I didn't realise that they were in love like that. Maybe I don't notice much these days due to being so in love with you. That's my excuse anyway.'

'They've been discreet so far, although they have no intention of keeping it a secret for long.'

Dolores and Jane had prepared a meal of a mix of Chilean and English dishes. The wine though was exclusively Chilean and had been brought by Carmen and Manuel; a red from the Maipo region and a chilled white from the Elqui province, not far from the town of La Serena where Carmen had been born and brought up.

'I've been working hard at educating Jane on Chilean wine. She might be an expert in psychology, but she seems to think that the best wine only comes from France. Unbelievable!' Dolores said, no longer able to suppress her laughter as she filled the four glasses.

'That's the sort of thing Dolores does for me. She drags me out of my staid approach to living, and not only with respect to food and wine. She has awoken a passion for life in me. I never thought I would ever be able to live like that,' Jane said.

'I reckon that I've gained the most, as I will be living with the two great loves of my life. Jane, who I have wanted to be with from the first time I met her; and getting the first good sized garden of my own. I have plans and ambitions to make a great success of both,' said Dolores.

She explained that there was so much more for her to do to create the cottage garden she was dreaming of. Her father had taken time to encourage and teach her when he brought Dolores to the garden in Antofagasta that he worked in to supplement the family income. She was a young child at the time and didn't take in a lot of what he told her. However, he had planted in her a love for growing things, mostly flowers and shrubs, but also herbs and vegetables.

'Maybe cultivating the garden will unlock some of that knowledge your father gave you so long ago. Apparently, long-lost memories can be triggered by the most unexpected things,' added Jane.

'I can vouch for that. Manuel and I have some good news of our own. We are buying a place together and hope to move in within the next couple of months. It feels right, although I never thought I would want to live with a man ever again,' Carmen said.

'We're a bit nervous truth be told, but it's reassuring to see how happy you two are with your decision to set up home together,' added Manuel.

'We're very happy. A few people don't approve but we've had nothing but good wishes from most of our friends and colleagues. The less supportive people are the joint friends of James, my ex, even though they must have known that our relationship had been a sham for years,' said Jane.

'Some people can struggle with change. It unsettles them, and they lose their generosity and tolerance. I reckon most people come round as it becomes ever more familiar, although some won't for religious or ideological reasons. Have you had any problems from our people, Dolores?' Manuel asked.

'No, apart from Javi blanking me. But what's new! Everyone was supportive after I told them about Jane and me, except him! Maybe he disapproves of same-sex relationships. I think he's an intolerant person deep down.'

'I think it's more down to him being so wrapped up in himself. If he sees no relevance of someone or something to the fulfilment of his own desires and ambitions, then he has little interest. I don't think it's worth bothering about, Dolores,' Carmen said.

'I can say this now. I never warmed to him. Recently, a colleague at work told me that Javi has split from Rachel for another woman at the university with whom he has been having an affair for some time. It's certainly not the first affair. Rachel is terribly upset,' added Jane.

'Having got to know him, and from what I have heard from others over the last few years, I don't trust him. I'm not sure what drives him. I haven't come across any other Chilean here who I feel like that about,' Manuel said.

Jane explained that Javi wouldn't be around much longer. He'd given in his notice at the university, the reason being that he was soon to return to Chile. He was not someone who had been proscribed, so there would be no problem on that front. Nevertheless, a lot of his colleagues at the university were surprised.

'Surely than can't be right. I don't attend those Forum meetings now, but some of my friends still do and they have said nothing to me about this. It sounds like he hasn't told any of them. I'm surprised he isn't on the proscribed list from what he claims to have done. When is he due to leave?' Manuel asked.

'He's not been specific about that, but his notice period is three months. So, in a few weeks' time, I would assume,' replied Jane.

'He always gave me the impression that he saw his stay in exile as temporary and that he would return to Chile, if given the chance. His relationships with women mirror that. He never wanted to put down roots here,' added Carmen.

'I still don't understand. Even if he is not on the proscribed list, how can someone like him go back to live under the military dictatorship? Is he going back to embark on some sort of underground resistance or guerrilla warfare? Somehow, I don't think so,' Manuel added.

Five weeks later, Javi boarded a flight for Chile. Before he left England, he told a gathering of fellow Chileans that he would always remain opposed to military rule and would work with others of the same view when he returned. He talked of being realistic about how long it would take to achieve change, although he emphasised that would always be his goal. He gave no more detail in response to questions about how he was going to achieve that change. He affirmed his love for his country and said he had never been happy throughout his years of exile.

Chapter 12

The arrival of children for Isabel and Pablo made their Chilean origins even more distant. Their lives had taken on a new dimension that left them with little time to spend thinking of not only the distant past, but even of the more recent past. In late spring 1988 they were compiling a list of friends and acquaintances they wanted to invite to their daughter's sixth birthday party to be held in their local community centre.

Both their children were in school and spoke nothing but the language of their peers, whether awake or in their dreams. Prior to both children reaching school age, the parents had spoken both Castellano and in English at home, but they had long succumbed to the futility of trying to resist the inevitable – that although their two children understood Castellano, they would only speak English. The fact that their children would grow up thinking and talking only in English was a matter of regret for Isabel and Pablo, but they realised it was not something with the degree of importance that it would have had for them in the early years of exile.

The children were treasured because their parents had given up believing that parenthood would ever happen for them. There was a prolonged period after their marriage when they were in despair, on account of two miscarriages and the subsequent gynaecological problems that Isabel had endured.

It was only when four months pregnant with the first child, after no serious problem had arisen, that they had revealed their secret to others. Isabel had told her women friends at the same time as Pablo met with Manuel to inform him. Their friends were told that if the child was a boy he would be called Manuel, and if a girl, then she would be named Carmen.

At the christening of the first child, the baby was named Carmen Villegas Otero. The second arrived less than two years later and was given the name Manuel. On the birth certificates, the parents included the surnames of both the father and mother in the naming of each child, but apart from that Chilean tradition, they knew that their children's lives would be very different from what they had experienced, not least because the children would not have Chilean nationality and would speak a different language from that of their parents.

There were many more people at the birthday party than had attended their wedding many years before, and the majority of them were English friends, accumulated in the fourteen years since they had arrived in Bristol. Isabel and Pablo seldom thought of themselves as Chilean, though they had never lost the longing to return to Chile, at least to see relatives and friends again. As the years rolled by, self-identification as an exile only surfaced on very rare occasions, as they were living a life little different from that of their English friends.

They had never been visited in Bristol by any relatives or friends. That was down to a number of reasons: the threat of not being allowed to re-enter Chile on their return, or being too frightened to fly, or their family and friends in Chile being unable to afford the long flight from the other side of the world. For Isabel in particular, a fear would often surface that she would never see her sister again. Pablo never talked of going back.

Among the Chilean community at the birthday celebration

in Bristol, the main topic of conversation was the forthcoming plebiscite in Chile that was scheduled to take place later that year. The result of that would determine whether the dictatorship would continue in power or if there would be elections held the following year to choose a democratically elected president. For everyone who had been exiled from Chile, this meant that at long last they were faced with a realistic possibility of being able to choose whether to return for a visit, or whether to live out the rest of their life back in Chile. There was no possibility of ignoring the significance of what was now on the horizon.

Towards the end of the birthday party, as the children played outside in the sunshine, Isabel took the opportunity to sit and chat with her closest friends on the matter which was on everybody's mind.

'Pablo and I were discussing it again last night. I'm less sure than he claims to be on what we will decide to do should the dictatorship be brought to an end. We are both looking forward to the possibility of going back and seeing relatives and friends.'

Isabel set out her indecision as to whether she would ever want to stay and make a life back there close to all those people she had never wanted to be separated from. That would be an upheaval for their two children, giving up a place and a life that they were settled in. She didn't know how any decision could ever be resolved to the satisfaction of everyone in the family. After all these years of making their home and building what were now lifelong friendships in England, she was unsure how she could ever bear to leave and return to a life that might only exist in her mind, albeit she had always retained a secret longing to live close to her sister again. She explained that Pablo could not see under what circumstances he would choose to move back, as it would be so difficult for the children which he considered would be unfair on them. Isabel's current inclination was that they shouldn't rule it out and that should the plebiscite and subsequent democratic election go how they hoped, they should not delay a decision of where they intended to live out their lives. It would be a lot worse were the children to be moved when in their teenage years.

'What are you each going to do should the opportunity to return come at last?' Isabel asked.

Dolores was the first to respond. She explained that it had caused her a lot of soul-searching. Her father was still alive as were some other close relatives so it would be great to be able to see them. The talk of restoring justice and truth in Chile had rekindled the memory of the massacre of her grandfather and other relatives, who had been among the thousands of unarmed men, women and children gunned down by the armed forces, in Iquique, eighty years before. There had never been any truth and justice for them and for decades the massacre was denied by Chilean governments.

'I don't expect things to be much different this time round, so I'm not hopeful for a good outcome.'

'So, you won't be going back even if military rule comes to an end, Dolores?' Isabel asked.

'Despite my doubts about getting truth and justice for all the killings and torture, Jane and I want to go back to see my relatives and friends. We won't make a decision on the longer term until we have done that. I still long to be with the people who I have never stopped loving, and I want them to get to know Jane.'

She confirmed that she was intrigued to see what life was like in Chile, as it must have changed a great deal from when it had been her home, all those years ago. If the plebiscite were to go the right way then she and Jane might go for an extended visit of about three months, starting not too long after the restoration of a democratically elected government, which was well over a year away anyhow. Jane was happy to keep an open mind as to the longer term and would move to Chile if that was what Dolores wanted, but it was difficult to imagine them deciding to set up home back in Chile.

'What about you, Carmen?' Isabel asked.

'I'm still in touch with my brother and I would love to see him, but as you know my parents are dead.'

Carmen explained that she had long maintained a focus on making her life here, rather than returning to the past. That had worked for her, but she had come to realise that couldn't work for Manuel and the victims of torture and murder, especially the relatives and friends of those who had disappeared, killed or tortured. She now realised that there could be no respite for them unless what actually happened was investigated and exposed, and there was some form of justice and reparation for those whose lives had been ended or been so badly blighted. So, now that there was a possibility of the end of the dictatorship, she had come round to the view that the past needed to be revisited and that the plebiscite might be the start on that road for her and Manuel.

'Does that mean then there is a chance of you and Manuel returning to live in Chile?' Isabel asked.

'Manuel and I have not made any firm decisions on that, and we might not end up of the same mind. He has some personal, unfinished business with his past. I now have a growing desire to help in any way I can in getting justice for the countless victims of the killing and brutality,' replied Carmen.

'We're still some way from the outcome of the plebiscite, never mind how all those big issues are to be addressed, if at all. I have been distancing myself from my Chilean past, especially since having the children, but the real possibility of change in our homeland has stirred emotions anew,' Isabel added.

At the bar, Manuel and Pablo were engaged in a discussion on the same matter.

'So, are you saying, Pablo, that you're definitely not going to return to Chile, other than to visit relatives and friends?'

'No, nothing is as definite as that. The plebiscite is not even certain, given there's always the possibility of the military cancelling it at the last minute. Should the outcome be a return to democratic government, then we will go back to see our relatives and friends. I just can't see how moving back there would work for the children.'

'Years ago, others returned with their children following the decree. It's possible to make a success of returning to live there with children born in exile.'

'The truth is I would prefer not to think about what decision we would take about a move back to Chile. I'm a bit nervous about how I'm going to react if and when we make our first visit back there. How does one reconcile what have been two separate lives: one before and one after exile?'

'Not easy, I grant you.'

'To see my father and brothers again will be emotional, but I try not to think about that as it might not happen before my father dies, given how frail he is. Let's hope the result is in our favour. But never mind what I think, what are you going to do if democracy is restored?'

Manuel set out his views on Spain, and the death of half a million people in the civil war there. In Spain, there was an abiding sense of injustice among the families and friends of those killed following the pact to forget, after Franco died. Of course the killing in Chile was never on that scale, but he couldn't bear the thought of such a pact to forget prevailing in Chile, although it wouldn't be the first time that forgetting or suppressing the truth of the past had occurred there.

'What do you mean?'

'Remember Iquique! Of course, the plebiscite and the restoration of a democratically elected government would be a good thing, but it's nothing more than a means to an end. I won't make any decision on what I will do until I see what a new government does about justice for the victims of all the killing and torture that has gone on since 1973.'

'That could be a long way down the line and may not happen at all. Even if agreement is reached on what happened before and after the coup, there will be contrasting interpretations on the motives, outcomes and the justice of what was done.'

Manuel responded by complaining that those with the power and resources usually had their view established as the official version of the truth. They had the resources to steer the educational system and flood the media with their version of reality. That reduced the search for truth to a battle for nothing more than public-opinion formation. Most people didn't have the necessary time and resources to scrutinise what they were told and what's more they'd never had the benefit of a good education to assist them to do that. All their energy and scarce resources were needed just to survive a hard life of nothing more than bare subsistence.

'Manuel, you're pissing me off. I'm meant to be celebrating my daughter's birthday and looking forward to the possibility of change in Chile. You are calling into doubt what we have longed for all these years – the opportunity to rid the country of the military, right-wing Government. Is there something else going on with you?'

Manuel admitted that there was. Carmen had been told that there was a real possibility that she would be unable to have children because of the damage done from the horrendous abuse when held captive. While Carmen appeared to have come to terms with it, he could not.

'Probably as a result, my nightmare has recently returned.

And there's also the bad feeling left after my mother died before I was able to return to Chile, yet my father remains fit and well for his age. Do I want to see him again, given we disagreed about almost everything?'

'You're right to be concerned about destructive feelings, Manuel. You don't want those to contaminate the happiness you've got with Carmen.'

'I know. I need to stop getting myself into this state.'

'Whatever happened to that novel you were writing?' Pablo asked.

'I haven't written anything for years, but with the potential for political change in Chile I am back on it and can see the possibility of completing it. Finishing the book was always dependent on the end of enforced exile, and hopefully the plebiscite in Chile at the end of the year will start that process.'

'I didn't know you had stopped writing. Why was that?'

'When Carmen and I got together, I lost the impetus. Up to that point, I had no expectation of any level of happiness and perhaps that void being filled with Carmen arriving in my life took away the reason I had for writing the novel in the first place. Carmen wanted me to continue, but I didn't. Until recently.'

'Well, it's good to know that there is a chance now of reading your finished novel.'

Part II

Return

Chapter 13

It was a momentous and unforgettable time. In 1990, the dictatorship ended and was replaced by the first democratically elected president for almost twenty years. Such was the joy among the Chilean community and their friends in Bristol that Dolores and Jane had decided that they would hold a party to celebrate, in place of their usual May Day party. In the weeks following the election of a new president, they had set about video-recording all the television news and discussions of the post-election celebrations in Chile. As well as their plan to show the video at the party, they had extracted all the press cuttings of the election about the new president and pasted them into a collage, which covered most of a wall in their living room.

Many hours were spent by them preparing traditional Chilean food such as empanadas, cazuela, sopaipillas and alfajores. Two cases of wine were purchased at considerable expense, comprising what Dolores considered the best Chilean wine to be found in Bristol. In the absence of any Chilean beer on sale in the city, they decided to stock up with Mexican beer, which they decided at least maintained the link to Latin America, if not Chile itself.

The guests began arriving in the early evening and were met with a flag of Chile pinned to the front door and loud, traditional music booming from the front lounge. An enlarged photograph of the new president had been hung from the ceiling of the hallway, but the one of the dictator, which had been taped to the wooden floor, was soon in tatters although still recognisable, much to the glee of the arrivals.

In the back room, the television showed the recorded celebrations in the streets of Santiago de Chile after the announcement of the election result. Pablo and Manuel stood smiling, their arms around each other's shoulders, holding beers, their eyes fixed on the screen.

'Seventeen years ago, I came down to breakfast at my parents' home to watch the coup unfolding on the television. What a difference to how I feel now. Have you been in touch with your family since the result was announced, Pablo?' Manuel asked.

'Yes. Raul was joyous, while Eladio was more cautious, though he did express pleasure that the dictatorship was at an end, albeit remaining sceptical about how much the new government will achieve. Are you optimistic, Manuel?'

'I tell myself to be happy with the president's announcement of the National Commission for Truth and Reconciliation, but it shouldn't be restricted to investigating only those killed or disappeared, with no naming of those responsible and no trials! How can that be justice? And no investigation of those tortured,' replied Manuel.

'You've always complained that the truth of the civil war in Spain was buried with that pact to forget, but this is a lot more than Spain has managed. Anyhow, there is the Amnesty Law that is still on the Statute Book in Chile. To remove that would require a new constitution. Do you really think that's feasible at this point in time?' Pablo asked.

'Perhaps I should be grateful for what's being proposed. It's certainly better than nothing and the Commission has been charged with producing a report quickly, within a year. Tonight, I intend to put my scepticism aside and shall be unquestioningly optimistic.'

'You'll need to get very drunk if you are to get anywhere near such an unusual state of mind for you.'

'There's a first time for everything.'

After eating, Carmen and Isabel spent most of their time in the front room where a few people were dancing. Carmen wanted to dance at some stage, but she was more interested in asking Isabel about her thoughts now on what the future held for all of them. She was still surprised at how interested she had become in Chile's future since getting together with Manuel, but her view remained that she would never want to live there again, even after the dictatorship had come to an end.

'Have you and Pablo thought anymore about going back to Chile?'

'No, we haven't. We want to see how things develop. In so many ways, we are happy with our life here. Surprisingly though, Pablo is no longer adamant that we should never return to live there. What are your and Manuel's thoughts?' Isabel asked.

'We've been a bit preoccupied after the miscarriage, but now that the medics are saying that there is a possibility of conceiving again, Manuel's mood has lifted. He's also more hopeful of justice being realised in Chile, but I wouldn't say he was optimistic about it. I am though.'

Towards the end of the evening, after most of the guests had gone, the group of friends had one last drink.

'To Dolores and Jane, for the finest celebration of a new era in Chile this side of the Andes. For the great food and wine, and the traditional music!' Pablo proposed.

'This has been a party worthy of the countless years of waiting for the end of the nightmare,' added Isabel.

'Thank you. Yes, indeed it has been a long time coming, but we have waited together. Jane and I are not going to Chile just yet. My sister is planning to come over here next year, so I'm looking forward to that,' said Dolores.

'I thought you were planning to go back much sooner. What has made you delay?' Isabel asked.

'It would be best if Jane were able to communicate in Castellano or she will feel isolated given none of my family speak English. We reckon that will take a couple of years. Also, I want to see how things develop. I still don't trust the armed forces. Will you and Pablo be in Chile at the same time as Manuel and Carmen are there?'

'Possibly! Pablo and I intend to go visit our families in the south. There are also a few friends I would love to see again.'

'I love the idea of meeting up with you two for some of the time there. It would take a bit of planning. I reckon we could do it, though. What do you think, Manuel?' Carmen asked.

'Was it planned that I would be the last to be asked, given that I'm not certain I want to go back yet? You three have already said yes to the idea, so what choice do I have?' Manuel asked.

'What's it to be, Manuel?' Isabel asked.

'You've got me drunk into the bargain, so how can I refuse with you lot of one mind? By next summer, the Commission's inquiry into the killings and disappearances that the new president has established will have published its report. So, on the basis of that welcome news, yes, I will be there in Chile with you.'

There was a loud cheer from the others which prompted Jane to put the music back on and the three couples stood up, faced each other and began to dance the Cueca. On this occasion, it was no longer performed as a bond with the land and culture they were exiled from, but as a joyous outpouring of an imminent reconnection with a long-lost love.

Chapter 14

'He's definitely not there!' exclaimed Manuel.

'Who's not there?' Pablo asked.

'How can he not be there?' Manuel asked, shaking his head.

'Who are you talking about?' Dolores asked.

'Roberto Almagro,' replied Manuel.

'Who's Roberto Almagro?' everyone asked in unison, apart from Carmen.

'You need to explain, Manuel. They don't understand what you're talking about,' she said.

Manuel explained that Roberto Almagro had been big in the party during the year leading up to the coup, and someone he and his friends had never seen again. He was older than them, someone they looked up to and sought advice from. Roberto Almagro was the person Manuel and his friends had been seeking when they were detained on the day of the coup. They had gone to his home only to be met with armed soldiers who were already there. The commanding officer had told them, or at least had given them the impression, that Roberto had already been picked up by them.

Jane, Dolores, Pablo and Isabel listened while Carmen went to the kitchen to prepare lunch. Manuel proceeded to describe how he had come to know and befriend Roberto Almagro.

He was a leading activist in the Socialist Party and someone Manuel and his friends thought highly of. He was more radical than Manuel, who saw him as a good friend though he always had an element of mystery to him. He recalled that Roberto never talked about his family, insisting that was the best way to protect them when the war began. When he asked Roberto what he meant by that, he smiled and said he suspected the armed forces would never allow the Allende Government to survive.

Manuel moved on to recount all that had happened to him from the day of the coup and in the weeks after when he was subjected to beatings and other forms of torture, which included mock executions. It ended with an unforgettable day when he found himself on what felt like an endless uphill drive in the back of a hot van without windows. He was weak from the beatings and believed the journey would end in his execution. During the journey, the officer in charge began to talk loudly to his colleagues of how he had killed someone called Roberto Almagro and how his body had been dumped at sea from an aeroplane, with his gut cut open so he would sink to the bottom. Manuel was convinced that was what was going to happen to him, but the journey culminated in his release at a border post with Bolivia, where he was warned never to return to Chile if he valued his life.

The Customs officers on the Chilean side of the border appeared to have been expecting him. On the Bolivian side of the border, he was met by people from the United Nations High Commissioner for Refugees who explained that they had been told that he would be released. They took him to the Customs building where his wife was waiting for him. She had been taken from her flat in Santiago by two men who showed their police identification and demanded she pack a few belongings and come with them. They had driven her to the same border post and told her that she and Manuel should never return to Chile.

Manuel had never been given a reason why he was released and that lack of an explanation caused intrigue at first then evolved into guilt after he found out six months later that all four of his friends, who had been arrested with him on the day of the coup, had been disappeared. In the years that followed, Manuel found out that three other party colleagues had also been told the same story while being held in custody – that Roberto Almagro had been killed and his body dumped in the ocean.

After those colleagues had been released, they reported what they had been told to the Vicariate of Solidarity – the Catholic human rights organisation which had been set up after the dictatorship had closed the first church-run human rights forum shortly after the coup. The dictatorship didn't dare risk moving against the Vicariate, which had been set up with the support of the then Pope. A great deal of the evidence in the recent Commission's inquiry into the killings and disappearances was down to the records provided by the Vicariate.

'Nobody ever heard of Roberto again after the day of the coup, so there was never any cause to doubt that he was dead. Until now, because he is not listed in the Commission's report. He is not on the list of those disappeared or the list of those killed. I have checked and checked again. He's not there,' explained Manuel.

'Perhaps that's an error on the part of the Commission. It could have simply failed to include information on him by mistake,' suggested Pablo.

'No that's not plausible. The Commission took information from every willing source and published what it had corroborated. My colleagues in Chile have told me that they checked with the Commission, and it confirmed that the information on Roberto Almagro had been provided by the Vicariate. So, an error can't be the reason Roberto Almagro is not listed,' replied Manuel.

'Then what could be the reason?' Dolores asked.

'The Commission report states that just over five hundred cases have been ruled out of the report because they did not fit within the terms of the mandate for its investigations. The only criterion listed which could possibly apply to Roberto Almagro, is that he is a person who had been reported as disappeared, but has subsequently been found to be alive,' Manuel explained.

'That seems extraordinary. Isn't that too far-fetched?' Jane asked.

'Not to me and my colleagues it isn't. One of my contacts in Chile has checked with the office of the Commission and it confirmed that the reason Roberto Almagro was not included in the report is because he is not dead. It also suggested that the name Roberto Almagro is an alias. It wouldn't respond to questions about Almagro's real name nor where he was living now.'

'You suspect he's one of those spies you told me of years ago, don't you?' Pablo asked.

'I do. After all, if he survived the killing and the torture, as it would seem he did, why has no one in the party ever heard from him in the past eighteen years? Why has he remained hidden? There is subterfuge in all this.'

'What will you do now?' asked Dolores.

'Those who operate in the underground resistance are determined to find him and find out why he chose to hide himself away. They have enlisted a few people who are well motivated and equipped to help track him down. We will see what that throws up.'

'So, you are planning to be out in Chile for a longer period to take part in that search for him, or perhaps even to find and confront him?' Pablo asked.

'Yes, a bit longer than Carmen. I will meet with old contacts to talk about Roberto Almagro and it depends on what happens with that. I will also be going to Antofagasta to visit Jorge's brother and sister. We should be in Santiago around the time Carmen is scheduled to fly back to England. Let's meet up then.'

In the following months, they met up on a regular basis to share their plans. Pablo and Isabel intended to spend most of the time in the south of the country, in Temuco, the capital of the Araucanía region, where Isabel was brought up and where her sister and family lived, and where she had some old friends she wanted to see. After that, they would go down to Puerto Montt at the foot of the beautiful lake region, after which Chilean Patagonia begins. The port city was where Pablo was brought up and where Pablo's father and brothers still lived.

'What will you two be doing, Carmen?' asked Isabel.

'Manuel will be visiting his father and sister who now live again in Valparaiso. How long will you be there, Manuel?' Carmen replied.

'No more than a week and possibly less. It will be good to see my sister. My father though is another matter. We clashed on political matters, so I don't know how that is going to work out. My sister tells me he is physically frail, but he knows what is going on around him. I plan to be in Chile for up to six weeks in all,' Manuel explained.

'I am only there for three weeks so we can't do everything together. While Manuel is in Valparaiso I will be seeing some old friends in Santiago before going onto La Serena, primarily to see my brother, but I may also meet up with Javi, who lives there now,' added Carmen.

'Javi has been in contact? Are you really going to meet up with him?' Isabel asked.

'He wrote to me through Jane at the university. Manuel is not keen and insists I should be accompanied if I go to see him. I got the letter last month saying he would love to meet up with me if I were ever to return now that the dictatorship is ended. He has lung cancer and does not expect to last the year. He says there are things he thinks I should know before he dies,' Carmen explained.

'How sad! Yet how intriguing! Even though I never liked him, it's so young to die and after all, he did suffer like the rest of us. I would be happy to come with you to see him if Manuel can't manage to. Pablo, is that okay with you?' Isabel asked.

'That's very considerate of you, Isabel, but there is no need. My brother will be around, and I have no fears about meeting up with Javi,' replied Carmen.

'In early August we can meet with you two and the children in Santiago, just after I come back from Antofagasta,' Manuel said.

'Really? That's great. How did you track Jorge's relatives down?'

'Through old contacts, but they have only tracked down his brother so far.'

Chapter 15

'You're asking too much of me, Carmen. I welcome the declaration by the Government that those listed as killed or disappeared had their human rights violated and I applaud the recommendations on reparation for the families, as far as they go. But you can't expect me to be satisfied until those responsible for the killings are named and brought to trial,' insisted Manuel.

'I understand that the Commission's inquiry is far from perfect. Don't forget that I, and thousands of others, who endured torture and rape, did not even feature within the terms of reference of the inquiry.'

'So what are you suggesting?'

'We must now fight for those to be included at some stage. That's my point. This is not the end of the matter by a long way. Yes, those responsible for the killings should be held to account and punished, but how can you then say it's right for you and others to take matters into your own hands and act outside the law?' Carmen replied.

'Those killers are still being protected. They wrote the constitution so that they retain control over what any democratically elected government can do. How can you be confident that this is the beginning of a process that will result in real justice for the victims when the armed forces have a right of veto on justice being served?'

'Nothing stays the same forever. I honestly believe that. It's for us and people like us to never give up pushing for justice to be fully realised. Those who choose to take matters into their own hands are as wrong as those in the armed forces they are accusing. Tell me you won't become one of them, Manuel.'

'I simply want to find out what I can from Roberto Almagro. I owe that to my friends who were killed for nothing other than their political beliefs.'

'Okay, but will it end there? You're getting into dangerous waters. The people responsible for the killing and torture won't put up with someone asking questions in an attempt to expose them.'

'Carmen, I have to know where my friends' remains are so that they can be given a proper burial. That's all I intend to do. If I walk away from doing that, I will never be free of the guilt that has plagued me. Can't you see that?'

'Fine, but I won't have anything to do with it. Please don't put our happiness at risk with this obsession of yours. Sometimes one has to leave things in the past where they belong.'

'I promise that I will not kill anyone. You have to trust me on this. Let's try to enjoy this flight back to our homeland.'

The pilot announced that they would be landing in Santiago de Chile in thirty minutes. There was no denying the unease that Manuel felt, as there were still doubts in his mind about whether he should be returning. Carmen was still asleep in the window seat, her head resting on his upper arm. He leaned over to give her a gentle kiss. She opened her eyes and smiled at him, as she slid her hand into his.

Manuel was thinking about the unique country he came from. Almost 3,000 miles in length and yet a lot of it not much more than 100 miles wide, sandwiched between the mighty Andes mountains and the Pacific Ocean, with every type of climate ranging from the driest desert in the world, the Atacama, down through the Mediterranean heartland, to a beautiful region with turquoise-coloured lakes and snow-capped volcanoes, and ending in the wild and untamed Patagonia, much of which was an ice desert.

'I'm excited, but also apprehensive about coming back. How about you?' Manuel asked.

'I'll just be glad to get off this plane and walk around freely. The thought of going out this evening to a restaurant in the centre of Santiago and being able to wander back to our hotel with the dictatorship gone, seems like a dream,' replied Carmen.

'It does. I want to stroll past the La Moneda Palace now that an elected president is installed there. It seems unreal to be able to do that. I can't remember going there often in the past, but I will never forget those images on the television of it being bombed and shelled on the day of the coup.'

'I remember being on a march to the presidential palace with Javi, but I can't recall exactly when or what we were marching for. That was before the coup, of course. I still struggle to remember so much of that period.'

'That's no bad thing. I sometimes wish it had all been erased from my memory.'

The plane was now flying lower than some of the peaks of the Andes, which were silhouetted against the bright blue sky. They held hands as the plane hit the runway with a single bump and they were propelled forward as the engines blasted into reverse. The plane taxied to the left and came to a standstill at the terminal building. When the engines were switched off, they turned towards each other in disbelief that they were back in the country of their birth.

The taxi ride into town was spent peering out of the

windows to see what they could recognise, but for some time it was all unknown suburbs of the city that had not been built when they had gone into exile so many years before. It was only when they approached the centre of the city that recognition of streets and buildings began to surface. They called out each street or building they recognised until Manuel fell silent when he noticed a street sign to the national football stadium. He could not keep from his mind that petrifying mock execution while he was being held there and he only managed to break the hold of that memory when the taxi pulled up at the hotel.

They booked into the hotel using their British passports, which they considered gave them a greater level of security than their Chilean passports. Manuel then ordered a bottle of champagne to be delivered to their room. After having a shower, they felt too tired to unpack and lay on the bed holding hands for a few minutes until Manuel got up to open the bottle of champagne and filled two glasses.

'To us, and to all those like us, who are returning to make their peace with the past,' toasted Manuel, as he clinked glasses with Carmen.

'If we are drinking the bottle, then we should also make love. Before that though I need you to promise me that you will not do anything that could end our life together,' said Carmen.

'I have no intention of doing anything like that, Carmen. Life would not be worthwhile without you.'

'You have to promise me,' demanded Carmen.

'I promise you that I will do nothing that would prevent us living out our lives together.'

'If you break that promise, I will never forgive you,' replied Carmen as she pulled him down onto the bed and began to unbutton his shirt.

'I thought you were tired.'

'I am, but we have to seal your promise by making love. I want you to remember all that you have to lose, if you don't keep your word.'

They strolled from the hotel to the presidential palace. For a few moments, they stood facing the entrance, turning their heads to look one way then the other, as if in search of something or someone they expected to be there.

'It looks pristine. Anybody who did not witness the bombing and armed attacks would never guess what happened here eighteen years ago. It's so easy to erase the past that underpins the present we are living in,' said Manuel.

'Isn't that what you say those in power do?'

'I think I might have described the media in that way. It is obsessed with creating ever new headlines and stories, while making little or no attempt to connect current affairs with what has happened in the past. Enough of all that! Let's go to the best of the many parks in the city, the Parque Quinta Normal.'

They both knew the way from Plaza de Armas, straight down Catedral, which was the often-travelled route to the park, but which was much changed because most of the shops were now unrecognisable. In their youth, the park had been a popular meeting place, with Carmen and Manuel each having their own memories of long sunny days spent there with friends, visiting either the Botanical Garden or the Natural History Museum, often ending up picnicking there or whiling away the hours on a boat, rowing around the lake. On their return to this much-loved place, they strolled for more than an hour around the shady pathways, stopping at familiar spots to tell a tale of a time spent there all those years ago. The only downside was the restricted views beyond the park, which was due to the much-increased level of smog in the city.

'What a place this is! So many memories and all of them good ones, but let's go to the restaurant as I prefer sensations to memories. Give me good food, wine and love any day. For me, those will always top good memories,' Carmen asserted.

During the meal, they went over their plans for the next three weeks. After spending a few days in Santiago together, Manuel would be leaving for a week in Valparaiso to see his family and friends. Carmen planned to stay on in Santiago for a few more days to meet with old friends, before leaving for La Serena to see her brother, and make contact with Javi, if he was still well enough. Before heading for Antofagasta, Manuel planned to return to Santiago from Valparaiso to do some research on tracking down Roberto Almagro. That would involve a visit to the Vicariate to examine what information they had and to meet up with some old party colleagues who were undertaking their own investigations. They agreed the arrangements for meeting up again for a final few days together before Carmen would return to England.

Chapter 16

It was a stormy day when Manuel arrived in the city of his birth, Valparaiso. The bus crawled down the steep streets through a series of hairpin bends, descending ever nearer to the seafront on the crescent of the bay. The view of the stormy ocean appeared less often as the bus snaked down through streets of multicoloured houses which hung precariously from the steep hillside that rose up from the shoreline. A memory surfaced of coming back on a visit to his hometown accompanied by friends, most of whom had been disappeared following the coup. His close friend, Jose, had been on that trip and that memory turned his feeling of warmth at the homecoming to one of sadness that he was all too familiar with. Jose had been listed in the Commission's report as disappeared, after being subjected to weeks of brutal torture. The lines of a Neruda poem came to Manuel:

> *I looked and there was my friend,*
> *his face was formed in stone,*
> *his profile defied the wild weather,*
> *in his nose the wind was muffling*
> *the moaning of the persecuted.*
> *There the exile came to ground.*[2]

---

2   Neruda, Pablo, 'El retrato en la roca', Alastair Reid, (trans.), *Selected Poems*, Penguin, 1975

His thoughts then turned to the poet himself who had lived for many years in this city, where he had died just a few weeks after the coup. Manuel had long shared the view that he was killed due to his iconic status as a supporter of the Allende Government. It was known that Neruda was in poor health at that time and that was the cause of death given by the authorities, but the absence of a credible explanation for the suddenness of his death was what convinced many, like Manuel, that Neruda had been yet another victim of the dictatorship death squads.

The hotel was within walking distance of the bus station. He had remembered it from his youth and decided on it because it was in the district where he most wanted to stay. He walked in what he thought was the right direction for some time before doubling back in the other direction when he failed to come across it. He could see nothing that resembled the hotel he had in mind. On asking a local resident for directions, he was told that the hotel had changed not only its appearance but also its name, with the result that he had already walked past it a couple of times.

He was shown to a room with a view along the waterfront, which had undergone a major transformation from what he recalled, with extended and modernised docks, as well as the much-expanded headquarters of the Chilean Navy. A sense of emotional detachment came over him as he surveyed the scene, in contrast to his memories of the seafront in his youth. It was only when he left the hotel and strolled up the steps of the old streets heading away from the sea that a connection with his past began to kick in. He stopped off in a café where there was a public phone. After the call to his sister, he took a taxi to her home on a hill on the outskirts of the city, from where there was an expansive view of the city and the bay.

Manuel was taken aback by how little changed Irena was. She looked only a few years older than when he had last seen her, almost twenty years before, and her enthusiasm and frequent laughter were undiminished. They spent several hours over lunch updating each other on their lives. Irena had divorced her husband many years ago and while she had gone through a couple of medium-term relationships since, she described herself to Manuel as happy with her present partner, although she had no wish to set up home with him.

'You are not the same though, Manuel. And why would you be, given you've lived so long now in England?' said Irena.

'What's different about me then?'

'You haven't changed that much physically, but you're no longer the brother who had so much passion to change things for the better. You have lost a lot of that optimism.'

'Well, I'm older now, though perhaps no wiser. I've had to change and adapt to survive. As to lost optimism, I can't deny that I have lost faith in changing things for the better. I am still motivated to get justice for the horrendous violence perpetrated by the State, but I suppose that is more about retribution than the beliefs I used to have about human virtue. Maybe that's what's changed in me.'

'Have you found happiness these last eighteen years, Manuel?'

'I have formed good friendships, and not exclusively with fellow exiles. In the last few years, I have found someone to love, and I have enjoyed the reassurance of being loved. So, yes I have found a level of personal happiness, even though it took a long time before I did. The distant past still causes me grief and depression, which I struggle with at times. Maybe I always will.'

'But doesn't the end of dictatorship resolve most of that?'

'It's positive news that it has come to an end, but that doesn't make right all the killing and torture.'

'Can anything make that right? I take the view it's best to look to the future and just be glad it's at an end.'

'Easier said than done for some of us, Irena.'

Manuel told Irena the full story of what had happened to him from the day of the coup to his deportation to Bolivia. He had long accepted that the friends he was with when taken into captivity on the day of the coup were dead. That had been confirmed in the Commission's report where their last known time alive was one of brutal torture. Their bodies had never been recovered by relatives, so they were listed as 'disappeared.' Manuel made no attempt to conceal the guilt he felt from being the lone survivor of that group of friends, and how he now believed that Roberto Almagro had been a source of betrayal. He was committed to finding him.

'Oh Manuel, how terrible! I never knew the full aftermath for you. If there is anything I can do to help, please don't hesitate. Like so many here, we didn't know – and some didn't want to know – of the extent of the evil that was going on.'

'I will pursue the exposure of Almagro. Thank you for your support, which I may call upon. But enough of all that dark stuff. What about the future for you? Children?'

'I don't suppose that's going to happen for me now. I have a job I like and a good income that means I can live independently. I have lots of friends and a relationship with a decent man who fulfils those particular needs. I don't need anything more than that to be happy, so I don't waste any energy aspiring for more,' Irena replied.

'Sounds like you've cracked it. I reckon women are much more self-sufficient than men. Not in all cases, but it's increasingly apparent as more women are freed from economic dependence on men. Having children does have great appeal for me, though it's unlikely due to the abuse that Carmen suffered while held in detention. I won't go into that as it's so awful.'

'From what you've told me, I like the sound of Carmen. As for children, where there's hope, there's always a chance, as Mum used to say. I like the idea of being an aunt.'

'And Dad? What has he said about seeing me again?' Manuel asked.

'He's nervous about it after all these years, but he is so looking forward to seeing you. He may have been critical of the Allende Government, but it did not make him a supporter of the dictatorship. He's an old man now and those clashes were a long time ago. Please don't get into an argument with him.'

'I promise, I won't. Of all the people I would want to take issue with, Dad is not one of them. I have no idea how he thinks now. It was always Mum who wrote to me and although she signed the letters from them both, I never knew which, if any, of the sentiments expressed in those letters were shared by him. After she died, there were only letters from you.'

'He could never write letters. He also finds it difficult to deal with feelings. He has to be in control and has never been comfortable with anything other than hierarchy and obedience. That's down to the Spanish ancestry, or perhaps his Catholicism. But you are his only son, and I don't think he ever stopped loving you, albeit in that limited way he can love.'

'You've changed in one way, Irena. You are a lot wiser than me. It's such a pleasure to be here and to listen to you talk. You must come to England to spend time with Carmen and me.'

'I will. I am looking forward to seeing more of you now, be that here or in England.'

The nurse led Manuel down a long corridor and stopped at the penultimate doorway. She knocked on the door but did not stay for a response. After a few moments, the door opened and there stood his father leaning on a walking stick, smiling, but with tears in his eyes.

'Good to see you, Dad,' said Manuel giving him a hug. His father dropped his walking stick while reciprocating in an awkward way. Manuel picked up the stick and handed it back to him.

'Come in, Manuel. It's been so long. How many years is it?' asked his father while wiping his eyes with a handkerchief.

'About eighteen.'

'Almost a lifetime! I hoped you'd come back when your mother was ill, but she knew you wouldn't.'

A feeling of irritation surfaced from long ago. He considered correcting his father by reminding him that it was not a matter of choice, given that when he had been deported from Chile he had been told he would be killed if he returned.

'I was sorry that I couldn't be here when Mum got ill,' Manuel responded.

'Could you not have made it for the funeral?'

'Dad, don't you remember that I was deported from the country and told not to return? I told Mum that in a letter sent not long into my exile. Didn't you read that letter?'

'I did, but would they have harmed you if you'd come back for your mother's funeral?'

'Dad, I was tortured and subjected to terrifying mock executions. I lost friends, who were killed by them. What would you have done in my position?'

His father began to cry. Manuel looked at him feeling a mixture of pity and irritation.

'I haven't come here to argue with you, or to offend you. I was too afraid to come back to Chile while the dictatorship ruled. Can't we leave any bad feeling in the past? I'm here now.'

'Yes. You're right. I'm sorry, but I still get angry about how our family was destroyed by all that happened. After all these years, still angry…'

'I can feel angry too, Dad. We share that. But I'm not angry with you. How about some coffee? I can make it if you want.'

Manuel was grateful to be doing something practical and taking a break from the conversation. On bringing the coffee into the sitting room, his father smiled.

'Irena told me you have a girlfriend you live with in England. Will you be getting married and having children?'

'More chance of getting married than having children. Carmen has problems with conceiving. We haven't given up hope, but it's uncertain. You'd like her – she's a much nicer person than I am.'

'It may seem strange to you, but I'd love to be a grandfather, though it probably won't happen now. Manuel, I always thought you were a good person. We just didn't view what was happening in the same way.'

'I'm more than happy to leave the past where it belongs. How about I take you out in the wheelchair for a walk. It's such a lovely day.'

They spent almost an hour in the gardens. They stopped at the rose beds, where Manuel's father showed his knowledge not only of roses but of gardening in general. Manuel had forgotten that his father had spent so much of his spare time in the garden, when he was young. His father explained that he was good friends with the gardener at the care home and that they planned and discussed the garden together. Manuel felt an admiration for how passionate his father still was about gardening. After they returned to his room he told his father that he would return again the next day to take him down to the old town for lunch.

'That would be great. I must ask you something though if you don't mind?'

'Feel free!'

'Will you ever return to live here? Not necessarily to Valparaiso, but to Chile?'

Manuel explained that he and Carmen had talked about that. They were keen to see how things develop in the country, but in all honesty, he thought it unlikely they would come back to live in Chile. After living in England for so long, their life together was there with close friends who had been so good to them. Nevertheless he and Carmen had not made a definitive decision, but regardless of that, now the country was no longer under the dictatorship they would always come back to visit their families.

'That makes sense to me, although I had hoped for a different response. As much as I would be happy to see more of you at this stage of my life, I can understand how your life is now elsewhere. I missed your letters after your mother died. I might be useless at writing letters, but I did like to read your letters.'

'I didn't realise that. I will start writing to you much more often when I'm back in England. I promise.'

'You've no idea how happy that makes me, Manuel.'

Every day while in Valparaiso, Manuel met with his father and on two of those occasions Irena accompanied him. There was an implicit assumption that his father now complied with, which was not to discuss the past. That meant they avoided discussion of the present political situation for fear of it taking them back to the past. On the last day before he was to depart and return to Santiago, Manuel was taken aback when his father raised a matter that Manuel never imagined his father had any awareness of.

'Manuel, I know it must be difficult for you to forget those close to you who were killed. If it was me, then I would want those responsible brought to justice and if that didn't happen, perhaps I'd do something about it myself. Don't fall into taking matters into your own hands, son. Tell me you won't do that? Please?'

'I won't, Dad, but I will pursue justice for my friends where I can. I couldn't live with myself if I didn't do that.'

'I understand,' replied his father.

Manuel was unable to say more for fear of breaking down. He could not recall his father ever empathising with him like he had just done. When Manuel met up with his sister for his last night in Valparaiso, he asked if she had spoken to their father about what he had shared with her. Irena assured him she hadn't. She suggested that their father had done nothing other than recognise a part of himself in his son, and in so doing he wanted to warn him. The next morning Irena accompanied him to the bus station.

'Should you need me, should you get yourself into any trouble and need some help, don't hesitate. Contact me! I will do anything you need me to do. I have an apartment near the docks which you can use if you want or need to,' whispered Irena as she kissed him goodbye.

Chapter 17

Shortly after the plane took off in the early morning for the two-hour flight to Antofagasta, Manuel took out the note that had been given to him a few days ago when meeting with a Party colleague he had known from before the coup. Written on the note was *Fernando Costas, Calle Bolivar 24, Antofagasta*. He was the brother of Jorge. His colleague told him that the search for Jorge's sister had been unsuccessful. At the meeting, they had also informed him that the pursuit of Roberto Almagro had thrown up nothing. The key to finding him was knowing what name he was living under now but after following up on a few potential leads, they were now beginning to accept that there was little chance of success.

Manuel was thinking of Jorge and how his brother would react when he turned up on his doorstep. Dawn had not yet broken so there was nothing of interest to look out at so he pulled down the window blind, adjusted his seat, and covered himself with the blanket provided. He was unable to fall asleep because of the discussion going on in the row behind. He could hear two young Chileans giving their views on their country to a Belgian man who was on an extended trip through South America. The youths were extolling the benefits of the dictatorship. Strikes never happened and their families and friends were now earning lots of money in what one of them referred to as the biggest growing economy in the Americas. Another of the youths spat out his hatred for *the communists* and expressed the view that with democracy restored there was every chance of those traitors wreaking havoc again, as they had done before the armed forces stepped in to save the country, albeit acknowledging that had happened before he had been born.

The Belgian was saying little but when he told them that he intended to visit the south of the country after his trip to Antofagasta, he was warned to avoid the city of Temuco as it was overrun with savage, indigenous people called the Mapuche, according to the youths. Manuel began to sigh and shake his head so he got up to make his way to the toilet and took a glance at the youths as he walked past. They looked to be still teenagers just out of school. On his return from the toilet Manuel stopped and turned to the Belgian.

'Welcome to this amazing country which has so many good people who have stories worth listening to. However, I wouldn't rely on these youths who probably still believe what they read in comics. Best to talk and listen to those who suffered and managed to survive the last shameful period of this country's history,' said Manuel as he smiled at the youths, whose faces were turning red. There was no response from any of them, though he was sure he saw a smile on the face of the Belgian.

Manuel spent the rest of the flight trying to come to terms with the fact that he had missed a whole generation that had grown up in a country which was so different to the one he had lived in. Of course, one had to take into account that those Chileans travelling by air would hardly be a representative cross section of the population and so the views he had heard could hardly be a reflection of the younger generation in the country. Nevertheless, the vehemence and hatred that the youths displayed, unsettled him. Should he be surprised given

161

that the dictatorship had taken absolute control of the media and education system? It was one more reason why he found it difficult to envisage himself living in Chile again.

In the early morning he boarded a bus to take him from Antofagasta airport into the city centre, which was several miles away. On one side of the highway the Pacific ocean stretched into infinity while on the other, there was a blistering hot desert stretching right up to the foothills of the Andes on the hazy horizon. But for the proximity of the Andes and thereby the occasional river valleys supplying water to the few coastal towns, there would be no human presence in this otherwise barren terrain. As the bus travelled through the outskirts of the city, the giant cranes of what was the largest port in Chile came into view. Manuel knew that it was here for over a hundred years, most of the world's supply of nitrates and copper had passed out of Chile. On his mind was Dolores' family and the many indigenous people in the north of the country who had toiled in either the mining or the shipping of these sought after materials bound for Europe and the USA.

After arrival at his hotel, the rest of the morning and afternoon was spent sightseeing. The city did not have the beauty and colour of Valparaiso on account of it being so industrialised and by the time he booked into a hotel, he was already wondering whether he should depart sooner than he planned. When he climbed into a taxi to take him to the address of Jorge's brother, he was immersed in fulfilling the long-held promise he had made to himself when Jorge died.

He was surprised when the taxi pulled up at a villa in the suburbs where only the better off could afford to live. There was a long gap between his knocking on the front door and the door being opened.

'Fernando Costas? I was a good friend of your brother who...'

'Who are you and why have you come here?' the man asked while he looked beyond Manuel to scan up and down the street.

Manuel gave his name and suggested it would be best to talk indoors. There was a pause before the man nodded his head and ushered him into the front lounge and told him to sit down.

'Are you Fernando Costas?'

'Yes. Who do you work for?'

'I live and work in England. I have done so for the last eighteen years. I am on my first visit back after all those years.'

'Have you proof of that?'

'Well I have a British passport,' replied Manuel handing it to him.

Jorge's brother looked at it and then stood up and strode to the window, looking out, again one way then the other.

'Listen, Fernando, I don't know what you are worried about but I've come only to tell you about what happened to your brother after fleeing to England. I was his closest friend there.'

'My brother caused untold trouble for our family. For years we were harassed by the police and the intelligence services. My father and I lost our jobs and had to turn up at the docks every day looking for work. Sometimes we got a day's work, others we didn't. It killed my father. Where was Jorge? Living well in England, I expect.'

'It wasn't like that at all. I'm sorry that you've had such hard times.'

'I don't want to hear anymore. Can you leave now.'

'I am so sorry. I did not mean to cause you grief. What about your sister? I'd like to tell her what happened to Jorge. Can you give me her address, please?'

Manuel was given a scrap of paper on which Fernando had

written, Teresa Garcia, Calle Sevilla 54, planta b4. He led him out of the room and as the front door was opened Fernando turned towards him.

'He's dead then? He never contacted us again after he left.'

'Yes, he's been dead for many years. I'll tell your sister what happened.'

Manuel stood outside in the road unable to move for a time. He then made his way down the road for fifty metres before stopping and then turning around. He quickened his pace back the way he had come in the taxi.

After picking at his starter, he decided against ordering a main course, but he ordered another half bottle of wine. It was difficult to make sense of what had happened. Perhaps Jorge's brother also suffered from mental health problems? If he did, how come he managed to live in a well-furnished house in a smart part of town? And how had he managed that if he had struggled to find employment for years after the coup? He came up with no explanations and wondered if he should bother to visit the address for Jorge's sister. On finishing the wine, he decided he should. If he got the same reaction then it wouldn't be so bad second time around, but what he could not dismiss was the chance that he might not. He would go late tomorrow morning as it was Sunday and therefore there would be a better chance of finding Jorge's sister at home.

The next day he was standing at the front of a block of flats in a very different district of the city. Across the street there were dogs growling at each other as they fought over the spillage from the tipped-over refuse bins. He made his way to the first floor and knocked on the door. A teenage girl opened the door. He asked if her mother was in and as she turned to call out, a woman appeared. She looked worn out and much older than he expected her to be.

'Teresa Costas? I am Manuel Caballero, a friend of Jorge. I knew him well, especially when we lived in exile in Bristol in England.'

'Come in, please. Would you like something to drink? It's such a hot day.'

Teresa asked her daughter to bring a jug of iced water and two glasses. They sat smiling at each other before Teresa broke the silence.

'Jorge is dead then. If he wasn't, he would be here instead of you.'

'Yes he died over eight years ago. He lived in exile for about seven years before that.

'And how did he die?'

'He was very ill in the end. His time in captivity after the coup was horrendous. He was tortured for long periods and that left him a different person from the one I had known back in Chile. His mental health had deteriorated. We lost him in effect. Perhaps like you did after the coup.'

'We never heard from him after that day of the coup. Didn't know if he was alive or dead, but a year later we were told by a colleague that he was in England. Nobody knew where in England. He didn't contact us so we thought he had forgotten us. Well, my brother insisted that was the case, but I never could accept that. It didn't fit with the Jorge I knew and loved. Now I know why.'

'I am here not only to tell you of his death but also to tell you in what esteem your brother was held by so many who knew him for what he was.'

'Was he looked after when he became ill?'

'He was. He was in hospital for several years before he died.'

At that point, Manuel saw that a tear was trickling down Teresa's face.

'I'm sorry but for all these years I have believed that you should know not only of his death but also be told of how highly so many people thought of him, for what he did in the struggle to improve the lives of people here.'

'And I thank you for coming all this way to tell us. All that doubt and hurt caused by no communication are now at an end.'

'I should tell you that Fernando did not want to know. He got very upset when I called on him yesterday to tell him all this. He didn't want me to speak of Jorge other than to get confirmation that he was dead.'

'Fernando is dead to me now. I won't go into detail but he went over to the other side. He lives well on being an informant.'

'I'd like to keep in touch, Teresa. Jorge was a great friend who I will never forget. I am not sure about where I am going to be living in the future but I will be coming back to Chile on some sort of regular basis now that the dictatorship is over. Anyhow, I like writing letters.'

'And I like receiving them, though I am not much of a writer.'

For the next hour, they shared accounts of how they each lived, managing to make each other smile and occasionally laugh. They were sure that Jorge would be very pleased with their agreement to stay in touch.

On the flight back to Santiago, Manuel had no trouble sleeping. Even the fact that he had met his first informant did not trouble him. It was another who was on his mind and unless he tracked him down, he would never be freed from his past.

Chapter 18

Carmen arrived in La Serena relieved to find a past that remained the same. As soon as she got off the bus at the terminus, she headed to the Plaza de Armas and sat on a bench surveying the scene. The colonial architecture was as it had been when she grew up and there was little in the centre of town that gave any indication of time having passed. That uplifted her after the long bus trip, much of which she had spent trying to make sense of her encounters with old friends in Santiago.

After Manuel had departed Santiago to go to Valparaiso, Carmen had been surprised by the unexpected loneliness that came over her, but she had expected relief from that when meeting up with old friends for the first time since the early 1970s. Within ten minutes of the reunion with each of her friends, Carmen began to feel she was in the company of someone she no longer knew. While sharing events and occasions from the distant past came without difficulty, when the conversation moved to how life had been since, neither Carmen nor her friends managed to offer anything more than a bare outline. There was a lack of confidence to reveal who they were now. The conversation often dried up after recounting what job they did and describing the place where they lived. Carmen found herself unable to talk about what had happened to her after fleeing Chile, or to talk of how she had struggled to survive and recover from the trauma. There was either an uncomfortable silence or a swift diversion to a mundane topic when politics came up in the conversation, be that politics in the past or in the present.

Afterwards, she had spent most of her time alone wondering why and how friendships could change so much. She was shocked that her friends no longer had the same political views which they had shared all those years ago. None of them had been as politically active as she had been back then, but she was sure they'd all shared the same values and sympathies. Carmen was left feeling bereft and then foolish that she had assumed all would remain as it had been, despite so much time passing.

It was only after arriving in La Serena and sharing her feelings with her brother Pedro that she began to make sense of it all. Pedro was a consultant in the local hospital and had only returned to La Serena two years before after many years living in Santiago. The move had been prompted by him splitting up from a long-term relationship and deciding he wanted a radical change from his life in Santiago. He so enjoyed living back in La Serena that he was sure he would stay there for good.

In contrast to Carmen's old friends in Santiago, Pedro was open and willing to talk and listen, not least about the political situation and all that had happened in the country since the day of the coup. During the dictatorship, he had been a volunteer at the Vicariate in Santiago and had supported the families and friends of those who had either been killed or tortured. He had recorded some of the stories of those who had come to the only organisation in the country which spoke out against the abuse of human rights. Those stories he recorded were of the dreadful things that had happened either to the person telling them or to a dead relative or friend. After listening to her brother recount some of those stories, Carmen was prompted to tell Pedro of all that happened to her. She felt assured and comfortable in revealing the trauma and sharing the challenges she had faced in recovering a life for herself. He listened without interruption, placing his arm around her shoulders as she told her story.

'Pedro, it's such a joy to talk to you. You're the first person I have met since arriving back in Chile, who is recognisably the person I used to know way before everything went wrong. It was so different with those friends I met up with in the last few days. I scarcely recognised them for who they are now.'

'Why do you think that is? Is it because they've changed or is it you who is so different?'

Carmen supposed that all of them have changed, which was to be expected, but she wondered why those changes had to cause such a great chasm to open up. She was unable to tell her friends anything of substance, and certainly nothing of the trauma she had suffered and how she had built a new life after that. She had picked up that her friends' political views were different now, but it was difficult to pin down why, as they didn't want to talk about anything that would explain the change. Life in Chile since the coup was a conversation stopper and after sharing memories of the distant past, there was little more to be said.

'This is no longer the country you knew. Some people have changed,' replied Pedro.

'But everyone must know what's been going on all these years. Some might be in denial and try to pretend it never happened, I suppose, but it's people abandoning their values and principles that I find so difficult.'

'Some of those who have gained from the last eighteen years may have had liberal views before the coup but now, out of either guilt or self-interest, studiously avoid talking about political matters. Others have embraced the propaganda of fear and conspiracy and now define all on the left as communists who want to destroy the country. The word *communist* is the equivalent of *traitor* to those people.'

'And what about those who have lost so much?'

'There are many who have simply been beaten down by fear and hardship. They have lost faith in their lives getting better through political change. A few have turned to guerrilla warfare, but the vast majority are simply devoid of hope and optimism. They spend all their energy trying to survive on poverty wages, with little or no public services available to help them.'

'I never realised just how different this country has become. I suppose those old friends I met up with in the last few days are those who have gained and feel guilt for having done so. I don't expect we will stay in contact. We have all lost so much, even those who think they have gained.'

'Carmen, you've dealt positively with what happened to you and come through the other side of that horror. However, there are many who have been embittered and lost any generosity of spirit, including some on the left.'

'The future has got to be better, though that may take a long time in the coming. Don't you agree, Pedro?'

'I do, but there are many wrongs to be righted. Despite what is claimed about the economy, there is widespread poverty with so many having no security in work, housing or health. That will take a long time to change, and I worry whether the extreme elements on both the right and left will allow that time.'

'Surely, it's more likely that the extreme right is the biggest threat?'

Pedro agreed but expressed his concern that the extreme left could provoke another coup by the right. There had already been several assassinations of former high-profile supporters of the dictatorship and although acknowledging that these were nothing in comparison with what happened in the years after the coup, he pointed out that the media, which was still largely in the hands of the right, was whipping up fear of 'the communist threat.' It was Pedro's view that it had been a great achievement by the new democratic Government to bring together both people from the right and the left, to sit on the Commission for Truth and Reconciliation.

In particular, it was noteworthy that all the Commission members signed up to the report findings, but how the few political assassinations since were reported in the media had resulted in the Government stalling on the changes that needed to be put in place. Perhaps those few assassinations were the tip of an iceberg of resentment at there being no judicial proceedings against those responsible for all the killing and torture by the dictatorship.

'Yes, the final and crucial part of moving on from all that terror is surely that justice must be seen to be done,' replied Carmen.

'I agree there must be prosecutions to achieve justice, but remember the military still have power in the Senate to stop that process and they could even mount another coup. With time I think there may well be prosecutions, but only after the power of those leaders of the dictatorship has been weakened.'

Pedro drove his sister to the care home where Javi was. A few months prior to Carmen returning to Chile, she had written to her brother asking him to find out what he could about Javi. Pedro had uncovered little other than that Javi was a director of a chemical engineering company operating in the copper and nitrate industries. From what he could find out, he had eschewed any political activism. Pedro had also found out through a fellow doctor that Javi had indeed contracted lung cancer and was not expected to survive more than six months.

Carmen fell silent for the duration of the car journey. She was deep in the memory of the times she had spent with Javi in Chile, questioning whether her feelings towards him had been transformed solely as a result of the terror suffered in captivity. She wondered if her feelings for him would have remained had all that never happened. Why had her trust in him evaporated so quickly? Was it just because he was a man and she'd lost trust in any man after the rapes, or was it, to some extent, because of the type of person she suspected he was? She was not sure which was the primary factor. The secrecy in his recent letter, when he confirmed that there were things he wanted to tell her before he died, had triggered a far earlier suspicion of his good character that she had long forgotten about. The car pulled up in the driveway of the care home and she took a deep breath as she got out.

'Remember to give the person at reception my phone number so she can call me when you're ready to leave,' said Pedro.

Carmen was shown to Javi's room by a nurse who knocked and opened the door. Javi was seated at a coffee table and Carmen went over to him and kissed him on both cheeks, as the nurse left the room.

'Thank you so much for coming. It's wonderful to see you, Carmen. And looking so well and as beautiful as I remember you,' Javi said.

Carmen noticed that his breathing was laboured, and she could see that he had lost a lot of weight, with his clothes appearing to be at least one size too big for him. She was taken aback at the condition he was in but was determined to conceal it.

'Who would have thought that we would meet up again in my hometown,' Carmen began.

'Yes, I remembered La Serena was where you were brought up. How is your family? Do they still live here?'

'Both my parents are dead, but my brother lives in the city. I don't think you ever met him.'

'I can't recall him, but my memory is not what it used to be. I don't know if that is because of ageing or down to the cancer.'

'Do you have family and friends around here, who come and visit?' Carmen asked.

'No. I don't have contact with either of my two brothers, and my parents are long dead. I have a couple of friends from work who call in most weeks. Enough of this small talk. I wanted so much to see you to put right whatever I can before it's too late. I know that what I am going to tell you will be difficult for you to accept, but please hear me out to the end.'

Javi started by declaring that for a long time he had worked for the secret police, DINA, which had been renamed a few years back. He had been recruited in his first year at university, before he had ever met Carmen. His job was to infiltrate left-wing activism and report back on what was happening and who were the leaders. When the coup happened, of which he had no prior knowledge, he was then instructed to accompany Carmen on her flight from the country. When they were both kidnapped in Argentina, he managed to get the leader of that group to contact his control officer at DINA, Roberto Diez, and as a result he was freed to return to Chile.

He was then ordered to return to Argentina, not to live in captivity as she was, but in accommodation nearby. His instructions were to appear in the courtyard as a prisoner from time to time, where Carmen would be able to see him from a distance, thereby continuing to think that he was being held as she was. In that period back in Chile, Javi had been informed that Carmen was to be released and he was told to accompany her to the UN refugee agency in Geneva, purporting to have been held in captivity as she had been. When in Geneva, he was to persuade Carmen that they both apply for resettlement to England and, after arriving there, he was to spy on the Chilean exile community, in particular, to get involved with those who continued to agitate against the military government in Chile.

'It was Pablo who first told me of the horrendous rapes, shortly after that embarrassing night in Bristol. Up to that point, I had no idea of the terrible things that were done to you. I had grown to love you more than I have loved anyone in my life and would never have been party to anything like that.'

Carmen did not respond. She stared at the floor with her head in her hands. Javi extended his arm to touch her, but she pulled away.

'After being told by Pablo of the rapes, everything began to change. I felt nothing but guilt for the brutality you suffered. I realised the enormity of what I had got myself involved in.'

'I don't want to hear this,' shouted Carmen.

'Please, Carmen! Just hear me out. I'm not denying it was a terrible betrayal of you and others who had done me no wrong but let me finish the full story.'

Javi claimed that he'd had no option but to continue with the DINA assignment for a while but decided that from then on he would feed back nothing more than innocuous information about Chilean exiles in England. He pressed for an end to his false exile for a number of years until at last DINA agreed to end it and permit him to return to Chile. Not long after his return he ended all contact with DINA, or rather its successor organisation, after it honoured the promise it had made to him, which was to get him a senior position in the nitrate and copper industry. That was the final pay-off and in return he was sworn to secrecy about his spying activities. He recounted how his choosing to live in La Serena was not only for work reasons but because Carmen had been born and brought up there, and his relationship with her was the only thing in his life that he valued.

He kept his secret for several years but could not rid himself of guilt at what he had done. It contaminated his life which was further blighted by the bitterness of broken relationships and recurring nightmares. He was convinced that long before he got cancer, his life was over and that any chance of happiness was gone. As a consequence, he decided to tell his story to the Vicariate in the hope that someday it would be made public and that the true nature of the dictatorship would be revealed when there might be a chance to hold the leaders, like Diez, to account. Javi pointed out that if Carmen read the Commission's report she would see confirmation of the surveillance of exiles overseas that went on during the early years of the dictatorship.

'Why are you telling me all this? As ever, it's all about you and your interests. You disgust me. Are you really looking for forgiveness? If you are, there's none that will come from me,' Carmen spat out in anger.

'I can't complain at your response. I thought it was right that you knew the full truth. I wanted to be honest with you, for the one and only time in my life, because you are the only person I ever loved. Something akin to my last rites.'

'Honesty? Why should I think you're being honest with me now? Why would I believe you when you tell me that things were as you've described? You're incapable of being honest.'

'I can only repeat that everything was as I have told you. There's another reason for telling you the truth. Years ago, Manuel told me of his feelings of guilt at surviving the coup when his friends did not. I knew about his recurring nightmare. I have some information for you that could help Manuel in getting some relief from that.'

Without waiting for a response from Carmen, he proceeded to set out what he knew of Roberto Diez, or Roberto Almagro as Manuel had known him. Diez had long been an infiltrator of left-wing organisations by the time that Javi was introduced to him at university and persuaded by him to sign up to DINA. Diez was by that time the leader or certainly one of its leaders. His skills at concealing his identify and his political sympathies were only matched by his loathing of 'the communists,' as he referred to everyone who did not share his right-wing views. Javi explained that Diez had become the torturer and killer-in-chief at a villa in Santiago where left-wing agitators deemed highly dangerous were brought to be tortured after being captured. Only a few were ever seen again.

'I know where Diez lives, or rather where he hides himself away. I would have thought that Manuel and his colleagues might want to know where they can find him.'

'What's in it for you? Why would any of us have reason to trust you?'

He explained that Diez lived on the western edge of Ensenada, a village on the shores of Lake Llanquihue, near Puerto Montt. The name of the house was Mirador del Lago. He lived there with his wife, although she was away working during the week.

'As to what's in it for me… let's just say a final act to bring some counterbalance to the many wrongs in my life. I reckon it will make things better for your life with Manuel. I know you love him.'

Carmen said nothing. She got up, walked to the door and left without closing it. Wandering for miles in a state of disbelief and growing anxiety, she found herself in the Plaza de Armas in the centre of town, where she sat on a bench, trying to take comfort in a place with a view that had never changed from how she remembered it. Carmen could not settle there and after a few minutes, she decided she wanted to be by the sea, to view the ocean of her childhood.

Walking at pace down the avenue, she arrived at the seafront and found the beach café by the towering lighthouse, where she had spent so much of her teenage years with friends. She scanned all the way round the expansive bay to the town of Coquimbo on the far side, before then fixing her gaze out into the Pacific. She focused on breathing in a slow, steady rhythm. After a few minutes, she felt in control of her emotions again and told herself that the only way to deal with this was to talk about it with someone she trusted. With some hesitation, she made her way to the public phone booth in the corner and dialled her brother's number.

Chapter 19

The bus swept into the terminus in Temuco, the capital of the Araucanía Region, and Isabel spotted her mother. She gasped and in that instant she realised that it was her sister, Paula. As the bus pulled up, Isabel took hold of her daughter Carmen's hand and rushed to the exit door, while Pablo gathered their hand luggage and lifted up their sleeping son. As the doors of the bus opened, Isabel ran towards her sister, throwing herself into her outstretched arms. They stayed locked together, swaying and sobbing and stroking each other's head, before drawing apart to smile at each other and shake their heads in disbelief. This was real – not the wishful thinking each of them had so often fallen into, down through the years.

'Paula, I haven't heard your voice. Say something!'

'We've come through it, Isabel. There have been times when I thought we never would. I can't believe I have you here with us, after what feels like a lifetime. And you, Pablo,' she called out, pulling him and the children into the huddle.

Isabel and Pablo's children held on tight to their parents, concerned not only because this was the first time they had seen them crying, but also because their parents were talking in Castellano, which they could only understand in parts.

'You must all be exhausted. Let's get your luggage into the car and get you home. How was the trip from Santiago?'

'As I have always remembered it, the last few hours in particular, following the Cautín River, with the mountains and snow-capped volcanoes of the Andes crystal-clear, stretching out to the horizon. I often wondered whether I would ever see that beautiful scene again. It's reassuring to see that the land remains as it always was.'

'Yes, the mountains and the lakes continue unchanged. Not so the city of Temuco! It has been transformed, as you will soon see. The dictatorship changed the country in lots of ways. It altered the way of life of so many, especially those who used to live on the land around here.'

Isabel was unsure what her sister meant but was not inclined to ask. On the drive through the city to their mother's house where the family still lived, Paula pointed out streets and buildings, only a few of which Isabel had a dim recollection of. She struggled to connect with what she was looking at, as so much had changed from the treasured memories of her youth which she had fought so long to retain. She felt the first touch of disappointment since they had landed in Chile.

As the car pulled into the driveway of the family home in the west of the city, the front door of the house opened and she caught sight of a middle-aged man emerging, slight in build, with greying hair, and walking towards the car hand in hand with two young children. Isabel assumed the man was Nico, Paula's husband, whom she had never met. The man looked much older than the one in the wedding photo which Paula had sent to her just over a year after their mother's murder. She had not cast eyes on that photo since the day she received it, as she associated it with the loss and grief at being absent from her sister's wedding.

'Welcome home,' said Paula as she turned the engine off.

After being greeted by Nico and shown round the house, Isabel sought refuge by turning her attention to getting her children settled. They had wasted little time in starting to play and explore with her sister's children. Isabel's daughter was talking with Paula's son in Castellano, which she had not heard her speak since she had started at school in Bristol four years earlier. After getting the children to bed later than normal, the adults took their places round the same kitchen table that Isabel had known when she was a child.

'I still find it hard to believe my eyes, seeing you sitting here, Isabel,' said Paula.

'In some ways the house still looks how I remember it, though it's better furnished and decorated than it was. You have made it lovelier than I ever recall it being,' replied Isabel.

'It's such a pleasure to have you and your family here with us. Welcome back to a democratic Chile,' Paula responded.

'Still confident that the new government will be allowed to govern without the interference of the armed forces, Nico?' Pablo asked.

'Yes, we are. We have contacts and friends in other parts of the country and they are also confident there will be no second coup by the armed forces, though they do exert a great deal of restriction through their block of seats in the Senate, which they retain under their imposed constitution. So, democracy is not under threat, but it's an imperfect one.'

'Surely it's impossible now for the dictatorship to stop the democratic Government making changes, given how the United Nations support it,' replied Pablo.

'To some degree, especially given that the USA supports the new government. There's so much to put right after all the wrongs of the last eighteen years, and god knows how long that will take, but let's leave talking about all that to another day. Here's to you and your children honouring us with your presence,' said Nico as he raised his glass.

'And let's drink a toast to our much-loved mother. She

would have been so happy if she was with us today,' added Isabel.

After the toast, Pablo explained how they would be spending their time. Following their first week with Paula and Nico, they planned to go to Puerto Montt for a week to visit his father and brothers, before returning to Temuco for a couple of days, and then spending a few days in Santiago prior to their flight home.

'How is your family, Pablo?' Nico asked.

He recounted how one of his brothers and his father had struggled financially for a long time now, to such an extent that they could not afford the fees of a care home which his father had needed for some time, due to his advanced dementia.

'Life here has been hard for so many. The rich have certainly got a great deal richer since the coup, but working people, and those even worse off who cannot find any kind of secure employment, live a life marked by hardship and insecurity,' Nico said.

'In the UK, Chile is held up as a shining example of economic success by the British Government and its supporters in the media. They claim that in the last ten years Chile has had the biggest increases in GDP of any country in South America,' replied Pablo.

'If the benefits of what is defined as economic success were shared around, then I would be inclined to agree, but that's not what has happened here. The regime created a paradise for the rich. It slashed taxes for the well-off and at the same time it criminalised trade unions, and thereby cut the living standards of the majority of its citizens.'

Nico went on to explain that Chile was a perfect setting for foreign conglomerates to invest in and make a lot of money from this resource-rich country, now even more so with such a low-wage economy. What a contrast that was with the

Mapuche people, for whom Nico did some legal-representation work. They had been robbed of more or less all of their land by logging companies. Nico offered to take them to meet a leader of the Mapuche community in the city.

'There are so many hidden stories about the reality here in Chile that need to be told to the wider world,' he added.

'We certainly want to understand how things are in the country, but let's leave those matters until tomorrow. Tonight, we should talk only of our families and the happiness of being here together, at last,' replied Isabel.

Early the next morning, Isabel and Paula walked arm in arm to their mother's grave. It was autumn and the fallen leaves would not settle because of the strong wind blowing in from the west. Isabel had agreed with Pablo that she and her sister would visit the grave on their own. As they arrived at the graveside, Isabel could no longer contain the tears that she had been fighting back since setting off from the house on the other side of the city. It was the first time she had cried for her mother since those days wandering the streets of Bristol, but there was none of the desolation of that time long ago.

'It must have been a dreadful moment when they handed you that death certificate, Paula. Especially given it had been signed by a person nobody was allowed to see and question. There was nothing you could do with the coffin sealed.'

'I never accepted what they wanted us to believe but there was nothing we could do. You have to remember that way back then the dictatorship was intent on exterminating anybody who opposed it, members of the Communist Party in particular, so Mum was in their sights.'

'Yes, everything points to that. At the time, you must have been completely bereft, with no recourse to any justice.'

Paula stated that justice was yet to be achieved, despite it being acknowledged in the Commission's report that DINA killed their mother. A few years after her killing, Paula had travelled to Santiago, to the Vicariate of Solidarity, to ensure that the killing was documented and known beyond the immediate family and friends. She had always held on to the hope that someday her killing and torture would be exposed. While it had been now, the fact remained that there would be no prosecutions. There had to be full justice delivered for the victims.

'I agree, but until recently we never thought that we would see the killing of our mother acknowledged by the State. Thank God for the Vicariate.'

'The people there were so committed to making sure the truth did not die with the victims. They recorded everything that I told them. I still believe there will a day when those callous men can no longer hide in the shadows, and there will be criminal prosecutions. I want that to happen in my lifetime, not as a footnote appearing in some history book long after we have gone.'

'I hope so too, Paula. I want to tell you about how I dealt with my grief. Shall we go for lunch? I don't need to spend any more time here. I always wanted to do this first visit to her grave with you as the final act in my grieving, but you have just reminded me that it can't be, without prosecutions.'

Over lunch, Isabel told Paula all she could remember about that week of mourning in Bristol. At the end of Isabel's account, they were both crying as they recalled the loneliness of being separated from each other at that time. They vowed to each other that they would never give up the fight for justice and to have the truth exposed for the thousands of others whose lives had been maimed.

Pablo lay awake in the early hours of the morning, while Isabel slept beside him. He was unable to work out why he had felt so ill at ease since their arrival in Chile. He had been spending as much time as he could with the children, not only to allow Isabel to spend time with her sister, but also to distract himself and to avoid any discussions and situations which he thought would exacerbate his mood.

On the first night in Temuco, although he had accepted the offer from Nico of a meeting with the Mapuche Community Association, since then he had worried about what he was getting himself into. As a consequence, he had decided to find a way of not going. After all, what could he do about the terrible things he would no doubt be told of on the visit, and would it not just depress him and leave him in a worse state? On his return from the bathroom, he found the bedside light had been turned on and Isabel was awake and sitting up in bed.

'In the last few days, I've noticed that something's not right with you, Pablo. You appear cut off and worried about something. What's the matter?' Isabel asked.

'I don't exactly know myself. I feel on edge. Perhaps I will feel better once we go and see my family in a couple of days' time. Maybe it's that I've still not returned to my Chile, so to speak.'

'There isn't a problem with Paula or Nico is there?'

'No, of course not. I like them.'

'And the children seem to have settled and are having a good time, so what's bothering you?'

'Maybe I'm scared of being pulled into something here that will overwhelm me. Something that will end up badly. It feels like I'm on the edge of a precipice, faced with making a choice one way or other, about where and how we live out our lives.'

'But that's not how it is. As we agreed, this is not a trip for making a long-term decision, and I've certainly not had a single thought about our future since arriving. Nor do I want to waste my precious time here doing that.'

'But didn't you say the other day that you and Paula had committed to fighting for prosecutions and getting truth and justice for those who were killed and those who were tortured but who survived?'

'I did say that, but it doesn't mean that I want to move back here to do it. Listen, I just want to enjoy being here, spend time with family and soak up as much as I can about this country. That's what you should do. Stop worrying about what the future holds and enjoy seeing family and friends.'

'You're right. I'm getting myself into that depressed state of mind again. You won't make up your mind about the future before sharing all your thoughts and feelings with me?'

'I promise, if or when that comes about. We need to see what happens in this country with democracy restored. Only then can we decide about our long-term future.'

'Okay, you're right. From now on, I'm going to be positive and enjoy the trip.'

The next day, Isabel and Nico went to visit the Mapuche Community Association that he did legal work for, while Pablo looked after the children. Nico had a meeting already arranged at the community association that afternoon. After completing their business, he was sure that the secretary of the association would be happy to meet Isabel and explain the plight of the Mapuche, and in particular what had happened to them after the dictatorship grabbed power in the country. On the drive there, Nico gave her a short history of the Mapuche since the Spanish Conquistadors had arrived in Chile almost five hundred years before. Although her mother had told her about the Mapuche, she had forgotten a lot and did not want to interrupt Nico's flow.

'What most people don't realise is that the Mapuche and their land only became part of the Chilean state just over a hundred years ago. Before that, they had resisted and had preserved their independence and their culture, despite constant pressure since the Spanish arrived in Chile. The Aztec and the Inca civilisations were defeated early in the sixteenth century, but not the Mapuche.'

'I had forgotten that. I suppose that means the memory of their identity as a distinct civilisation must be more alive and vivid, quite different from those long-lost worlds of the other Andean civilisations destroyed by the Spanish Conquistadors.'

'Exactly! What has happened during the dictatorship, I will leave Jose, the secretary of the association, to explain to you.'

While Nico conducted his business in a back room, Isabel got talking to people who were calling in to seek advice on a variety of legal and welfare matters. It brought to mind why she liked being a social worker, as engaging with people about their problems was something that came easily to her. She became immersed in listening to the issues that people were concerned with, largely the loss of their land and their homes, but also the resultant lack of secure employment to provide a steady and reliable income. Towards the end of the afternoon, Nico emerged from his meeting and invited Isabel to join him in the back room.

'Welcome, Isabel. Nico tells me this is your first visit back after escaping all those years ago, and that you are keen to learn what has been happening to the Mapuche since you left,' said Jose, as he smiled and shook her hand.

'Sitting in your reception, I've been hearing a lot of stories that have shocked me, so yes I'd like to understand the overall picture of how it has all come to be,' replied Isabel.

'In a nutshell, we had more or less all our land taken from us by the dictatorship. We had been losing land for hundreds of years, but these last years have been devastating. In 1973, Mapuche people owned ten million hectares of land in our last refuge in this region of Araucanía; now that has been cut by ninety-five per cent to a mere 500,000 hectares.'

'How has that happened? Who owns the land now?' Isabel asked.

Jose explained that the military government had instituted decrees that took possession of vast tracks of land, evicting the Mapuche owners who had earned their living from it, and granting that confiscated land to mostly foreign forestry and logging companies, in which rich Chileans had shares. Logging was now a multimillion-dollar industry in the region. To add insult to injury, the Mapuche people on the remaining five per cent of their ancestral lands were struggling to cultivate it and had to abandon much of it, due to the logging companies using up so much of the water resources on which those smallholders depended. Although there had been resistance, some of it violent, the community had not managed to stop or even slow down the haemorrhage of land from Mapuche people, who had been given only paltry compensation for their loss, and in most instances none at all.

'So how have those thousands of people been able to make a living after being evicted from their land?'

Jose leant back in his chair and began. Many of the men had moved away and constantly travelled around this vast country to find work. When they did get work, it was poorly paid and insecure. Often the work ended after only for a few days. The little money they had left over after accommodation and food had been paid for, was sent back to their families. Some of those who had remained in the region earned what they could doing occasional and temporary work for the very forestry companies that now possessed their land. Jose claimed that what the State wanted to do was to break Mapuche communities and families, but he believed that would not be achieved because his people would never give up the fight for the return of their land.

'My mother would be heartened by your resistance.'

'I know she would, Isabel. My mother was good friends with her. Your mum was a great friend to our community. Let me tell you what I know of her.'

Jose explained that like most Indigenous people, his family had been dirt poor and on many occasions had been dependent on a local charity to get by. Isabel's mother had regularly done voluntary work for that charity to support the parents of Mapuche children to keep their children in school, rather than have them leave to work and earn what little they could to contribute to keeping the family fed and clothed. He recounted that his mother had told him that Isabel's mother made a substantial payment to the charity from her salary every month. Those payments had been made for more than fifteen years, right up to the time when she was killed.

It was only then that the generosity of her mother was linked in her mind to a matter that had been a source of irritation to Isabel when she was a child. It was that her mother never spent much money on her sister and herself, certainly in comparison with other families they knew, some of whom were no better off, and in many cases worse off than her family. Tears welled up in her eyes.

'Isabel, I'm sorry. I didn't mean to upset you,' Jose responded.

'You haven't upset me, Jose. You have made me even more proud of my mother than I was.'

On the drive back, Isabel asked Nico for his thoughts on the future, in the light of all that Jose had said about the plight of the Mapuche. Nico's view was that the scale of the problem was so great that any solution would take a very long time to be achieved, if at all. To reverse all the injustices which had started at least a hundred years before the military coup, although the military regime had accelerated those injustices, would require concerted action over many years just to restore half of the ancestral land that the Mapuche were demanding. The forestry and logging companies, who now had possession of that land, were powerful and well-connected and would demand compensation that no government sympathetic to the Mapuche cause could pay. On the other side of the divide, the history of the Mapuche people showed that they would never give up their fight, not only for the return of their ancestral land, but also for autonomy, if not independence, from the Chilean State.

'It all sounds beyond redemption, Nico.'

'The election of a democratic government is nothing but a tiny step on a long journey but at least with the end of the dictatorship, the lengthy process of undoing the systematic injustice can perhaps start. We can't change the past, but one must be optimistic when thinking of the future. Wouldn't you agree?'

'That sounds about right. I'm certainly beginning to realise that my future is nowhere as daunting as that faced by others.'

'Is your future daunting, Isabel?'

'I think it might be for some of us who fled this country. The reason for continuing in exile no longer applies with the ending of the military regime, which raises the question of returning or not. It's not only the country that has changed. We have all changed while in exile.'

'So, what will you decide to do?'

'Pablo and I don't know. We've agreed not to consider the matter until we see what happens and we understand this country better. The children are settled in England and it's what they've always known, so it would be a big decision to leave our life there and come back to Chile. I think it's unlikely, but it's a possibility.'

'It's ironic that optimism about the future of the country also brings hard personal decisions for those exiled for so long. Whatever you decide, you should know that our financial position is much better than it was. Paula is working now, and I'm earning more than I was. That means we could visit you in England from time to time, if you do decide to continue living there.'

'That's helpful to know, Nico. I couldn't face being separated from my sister again for years on end.'

Isabel looked out of the bus window on her way to the centre of town, where she had arranged to meet up with her old friend, Maria. Since she had arrived in Chile, her mood had spanned elation at being able to talk to and do things together with her sister after living so long apart, to feelings of uneasy detachment from the city in which she had been born and brought up. Temuco had grown to such an extent that the population was now well over twice the size it was when she had lived there. Even the old city centre, now with several high-rise buildings, was for the most part unrecognisable from what she had known and loved. What's more, the family home which was once on the edge of the city with unbroken views across the meadows to the river, had been swallowed up in vast new housing estates and was now far from the setting it used to be, where the conurbation came to an end and the countryside began. It no longer had the emotional attachment that she had held onto, right up to arriving at the front door almost a week ago.

The past week had also brought home to her the transformation in herself. She was no longer that person who didn't wish to know anywhere other than the city of Temuco where she lived. That realisation was followed by a sense of guilt. She didn't want her sister to know of these feelings, nor did she want to bother Pablo with them, as she was worried that they might add to his struggle to come to terms with his own dislocated state of mind. She would be relieved to distance herself from the city she had grown up in, when they departed the day after tomorrow for Puerto Montt, to visit Pablo's family.

After getting off the bus in the city-centre bus terminus, she made her way to a café which Maria had given her directions for over the phone. On entering, she looked around and recognised nobody, so she took a seat at a table near the entrance. It was then that she caught sight of a woman in the far corner by the side window, getting up from her table with some effort and walking with a pronounced limp towards her. As the woman approached, she recognised Maria, who smiled at her through the tears in her eyes.

'You're still recognisable, Isabel. What a joy to see you again.'

'Maria! It's been so long,' replied Isabel, hugging her, while intent on hiding the shock at how her friend had aged.

'Yes, much too long. So much has happened in both our lives, I'm sure. I'm glad you got out, Isabel. Had you not, I doubt you would be here with me today.'

'Paula told me about Juan, and I saw the paragraph on him in the Commission's report. I am so sorry, Maria. Such a loss for you and the children, but also for the rest of us who so admired his courage and commitment. I can't imagine how hard it has been and must still be for you.'

'Just look at me! I can't deny it hasn't taken its toll, but for as long as I live, I shall remain in hope that there will be some justice, for Juan and the thousands of others who were tortured or killed. Many others in my situation have little belief in justice, but I feel I would be betraying Juan if I didn't, but you don't want to listen to me going on about my life. How are you doing?'

'I want to hear how it has been for you. I want to know the truth and if anybody's story should be told, it's yours. So, if you can bear it, please tell me. I want to hear all that you've gone through and how you still manage to retain that optimism. Of course, if you'd prefer not to, I will understand.'

'That's how I have always remembered you, Isabel. Honest and persistent, just like your mother! Okay, I'll tell you how it has been.'

The last day Maria had seen Juan alive was when he'd left their home for work on a morning like any other. When he did not return in the evening she began to worry. The next day she arranged for her aunt to look after their two young children while she started the search for her husband by phoning the local police headquarters in Temuco. They showed no interest, so she then went to the police headquarters building demanding answers. After a few days of continuously parking herself in the reception area, they told her that SICAR, the police intelligence service, had no record of her husband being detained and that it had checked with the Army Intelligence Directorate, but it also said it knew nothing of her husband. Later that same day, a colleague of Juan's called at her home to say that he had seen him being bundled into a black van by three armed men in balaclavas, at the entrance of the community association where they worked.

For over a year she heard nothing more until another friend of Juan's called at her home one evening to tell her that a member of the Socialist Party in Temuco had reported that he'd seen Juan when he had been held during the previous year in Villa Grimaldi in Santiago, the assumed headquarters of DINA. The party colleague had been released after several weeks of torture, but he'd seen Juan in a poor state being dragged to what was called 'the Tower,' which was where prisoners were held in very cramped cages in solitary confinement, with only enough room to crouch down. There was no known case of anyone who was taken there ever being seen again. It was then that Maria accepted that Juan was dead – 'disappeared' as so many others had been. The authorities continued to issue denials of any knowledge of Juan being arrested, tortured or killed, all of which consolidated Maria's view that they knew full well what had happened to her husband and the father of her children.

'Maria, what you have been through all these years!' Isabel managed to say in a faltering voice. She tried hard not to cry and make things worse for Maria.

'Yes, those first few years after his disappearance were traumatic. I would never have got through them without the help of my aunt and other friends and relatives. Those people not only looked after me and the children, but they funded us for years until I got a job, after the children started school. All that generosity despite them having little to live on themselves.'

'Yes, Paula told me. It's a credit to who you are that you got through those bleak times.'

'I sometimes think of it as a miracle, given what the repercussions have been. Being disappeared brings many problems for those left behind.'

Maria explained that as Juan could not be declared dead without a body being found, she had no entitlement to any life insurance or any pension. The family lost its home and moved in with her aunt. But it did not end there. Mental-health problems followed on and it was only a local charity that saved her when it paid for the treatment she needed.

'As you can see, my physical health has also suffered. You can tell that by how old and frail I look for someone who is in their early forties. The children's education has suffered too as there has been no way of affording to pay for the university education which their exam grades qualified them for.'

'The Commission has made a number of recommendations on reparation to victims such as yourself, Maria. They appear to address in a small way all the suffering you have gone through. I suppose that is at least a little recompense for what can never be made right.'

'Yes, if the Government does all that the Commission recommends then it will be of great help to me and the children, but I have learned not to rely on anything until it actually happens. I am hopeful though.'

'And yet, you are still managing to maintain optimism in the future. You're an incredible person, Maria. We must stay in touch and when the time is right we will fund you and the children to come over to spend a holiday with us in England, although that might not appeal to you just yet. That offer will always remain open for you to take up.'

'I promise to take you up on that sometime in the future, but only when there has been some progress on justice and reparation here. I want to do what I can to press for that, together with so many others who will never allow these crimes to be forgotten.'

When Isabel got back, she told Pablo everything. He sat with his head bowed for much of it and at the end he raised his head to stare at the wall. All of a sudden he banged his fist on the table, which startled Isabel.

'That's what I'm frightened of. Hearing about how horrendous life has been for people like Maria. It stirs a rage inside me, which scares me. We should do what we can for Maria and those like her who have an anguish that they can never be rid of. Such heartless cruelty!'

'Yes we should, but we need to work out what that means in practical terms. And that does not mean we should move back to this country. Tomorrow, we're going down south to see your family. Probably, there will be more stories of suffering there. Are you going to be able to cope with that?'

'There will be more hardship stories, but my family is alive, and none of them has suffered like Maria. I've been hiding myself away from all the pain and guilt about what has gone on here. No longer! I am going to enjoy seeing my family.'

'I've felt that guilt too and for a period this afternoon it was almost overwhelming, as I listened to Maria. But I am determined not to waste my energy on feeling guilty. I didn't torture or kill anyone, and I certainly didn't abandon my country. It abandoned me.'

Chapter 20

Pablo saw it long before the bus reached the lakeside and parked to allow the passengers a break before the final leg of the journey to Puerto Montt. On the distant shore of Lake Llanquihue, Osorno, the snow-capped volcano, rose as a perfectly formed cone to almost 9,000 feet. For Pablo, Osorno would always be the most beguiling wonder of the world, and in his opinion even better when viewed further east from the Petrohue waterfalls of the turquoise waters of Lake Todos los Santos. He was transfixed, convinced that he had returned to the best of what he had known in his childhood. He took deep breaths of the pine-scented air from the wooded slopes that surged upwards from the shores of the lake on every side, and he marvelled at how the beauty of this scene had not faded, unlike human beauty that starts to decay not long after it has reached its zenith.

All too soon it was time to move on. Pablo stayed silent as the bus crawled up the hill, departing from the lakeside town of Frutillar on the final stretch of the journey to Puerto Montt. Isabel saw that he wanted to be left with his own thoughts and feelings, so she engaged the children in reading from a storybook in the row of seats in front of where he sat alone.

His memory was as sharp as the clear air that was enabling him to see for miles into the distance, locked onto the time when he was a child, sitting by his mother's side on a bus trip leaving the lakeside town of Frutillar on a day such as this. His mother was coughing a lot. She must have already been very ill at that point. She died almost four months later. He could not recall returning to this area until he was in his early twenties, because he had come to associate it with his mother's death. It was only when he fell so madly in love with Isabel that he decided to see if he could break that association by going there with her. That weekend trip restored all the lost love he had for the place.

Sitting on the bus almost twenty years after that redeeming episode, Pablo was so immersed in those memories that he did not notice that they were now entering the outskirts of Puerto Montt, the city where the Pan-American Highway ends and Chilean Patagonia begins.

'We're almost here, Pablo. You look as if you're somewhere else,' said Isabel.

'Yes, I was on that first journey to Lake Llanquihue with you. Do you remember that?'

'I do. That was when we first made love, or have you forgotten that?'

'How could I ever forget?' Pablo replied with a smile.

Pablo's brothers, Raul and Eladio, were standing behind the barrier at the bus station, one with his hands in his pockets and the other shielding his eyes from the setting sun. Pablo recognised them in an instant, as the bus swung into the bus station. They looked much older, but there was no doubt it was them. He rose from his seat and felt his throat tighten as he stared at them through the window.

'You go, Pablo. I'll bring the children,' said Isabel.

His brothers recognised Pablo as soon as he stepped down off the bus and they all broke into a run towards each other.

They collided in a powerful hug, patting each other on the back and then stepping back to look at each other before hugging again.

'Pablo! Pablo!' was all that the brothers could say.

'This is a dream! Ever since I was exiled from here I've been too scared to think about this day. I thought that if I did it might mean it would never come to be. Yet now I'm with you, and here's Isabel with our children, Carmen and Manuel,' Pablo managed to say before his voice broke.

Raul and Eladio hugged and kissed them all in turn before Eladio carried all their suitcases to the car.

'I'm sorry that neither I nor Eladio have a big enough place to accommodate you, but I'm sure you will be pleased with the place we have found for you,' said Raul.

'There's nothing for either of you to be sorry about. How's Dad?' Pablo asked.

'Good news! Last week he was moved to a care home. After years of waiting, a charity has agreed to fund it. He's very frail now and he does not recognise any of us, but he seems happy in the home,' replied Raul.

'That's great. It must be a big relief for you both. I'm so grateful to you and your wives for caring for him all this time he has been unable to manage on his own.'

'And we're grateful to you for the money you sent us. It has been a big help in being able to pay for some outside care, especially for Ana and Rosa, as they've been doing most of the caring.'

They were driven to the house that the brothers had rented for Pablo's family for their weeklong stay. It was located in an elevated position overlooking the harbour and the bay, with the mighty Pacific opening up beyond. For a few moments, the three brothers stood at the edge of the drive, locked arm in arm, gazing out at the view, before hugging again and then turning towards the front door of the house. After showing Isabel and Pablo around the house which they had stocked with provisions, the brothers departed, saying they would return around seven o'clock with dinner, which their wives had prepared.

'They're so kind, Pablo. I know they struggle to make a living, yet they have spent so much on making us feel at home. Shouldn't we offer to reimburse them?' Isabel asked.

'I think that would offend their dignity. Better to take them out for a meal a couple of times, and get some presents for the children,' replied Pablo.

'Let's do that then. Your family has always been so kind. Isn't it heart-warming to see that hasn't changed?'

'It is. Undoubtedly, things have been hard for them, especially Eladio, but we will hear more about that during the coming week. I feel so good being here. Surprisingly good!' Pablo said, before going upstairs to check the children were okay.

His brothers and their families arrived just before seven o'clock. Ana and Rosa wasted little time in making the final preparations before the six adults and five children sat down round the large dining-room table, to eat a meal that they were proud to state comprised nothing but local produce. A short time after the meal ended the children were encouraged to go to another room to play, leaving the adults around the table.

'I haven't had fish like that since I lived here. Of course, we have fish in Bristol and the city is close to the sea, but I just don't think the fish is as fresh as it is here. Did you catch that on your boat, Raul?' Pablo asked.

'Yes. Until recently, fishing was a good business to be in on the back of the hugely expanded fish-processing industry that took off in a big way after you left, Pablo. The demand for fish from the fish-processing companies increased so we were able to get a good price, but that's changing now,' explained Raul.

'Why now?' Pablo asked.

'Salmon farming is now the expanding industry around here. That's reducing demand for wild fish from fishermen such as myself, but the more worrying, longer-term effect is the pollution it is causing. Already, there has been a noticeable drop in natural fish stocks around the coast. I worry about my future, but Eladio has had to put up with a lot worse,' replied Raul.

'Pablo, I'll tell you about that before you go, but not tonight, when we're celebrating your return. I am glad you fled after the coup as you would have ended up dead had you stayed. Your tendency to react to any injustice you came up against would surely have got you killed,' Eladio added.

'And right from an early age. Dad used to say how you had a nature of extremes: kind and placatory most of the time, but when you thought you or others were being unfairly treated, you would get so angry – even explode at times. Are you still like that?' Raul asked.

'No, I don't think I live in those extremes now. I don't know how much that has to do with where I live or if it's because I've changed or matured with age. Maybe I've become a duller, less caring person, as I've got older,' replied Pablo.

'I didn't know you were like that when young, Pablo,' Isabel added.

'We can tell you lots of stories of Pablo getting into fights in the playground, and outside school. If any of his friends were bullied or picked on, he would fly into a rage which came as a shock to those he fought with, given he was so easy-going otherwise,' added Raul.

'I think you're exaggerating a bit, but I won't deny that I could get into a fury sometimes.'

'Surely that's why you became a political activist and got involved in trade unionism when you started work,' Eladio said.

'Perhaps! I don't fly off the handle now though, do I, Isabel?'

'No, I've never seen you do that. It's a bit hard to think of you as the angry young man. I knew you were committed to the same things I felt strongly about, but I never saw that rage you had when younger.'

'Eladio and I weren't like Pablo, although I was a bit envious of his courage. I used to wish I could have been more like him,' added Raul.

'It wasn't courage. I can remember the first fight when I was so scared of being beaten up by this older kid that I went crazy and lashed out at him and didn't let up. I managed to win the fight and was as surprised as any of the others who saw that. So, I got a reputation as a fighter. Every fight after, I never lost that fear and lashed out as if I was crazy.'

'Well, whatever the reason, it did continue beyond your childhood. Perhaps less of the physical fighting, but you never stood idly by when trouble came for you or your friends. Here's to us, the brothers, and the great women we have been lucky enough to have in our lives,' said Eladio as he raised his glass.

On the Sunday, the three brothers went together to see their father in the care home. In the back seat of the car, Pablo tried to work out when was the last time he had seen his father. He decided it was four days before he fled Chile with Isabel, after they had heard they were being sought by the police for questioning. At that time, they were living in Temuco but had gone into hiding at a friend's house, so Pablo had decided to make the journey to see his father and brothers before leaving the country. When he arrived in Puerto Montt, he went to see his brother first who told him the police had turned up at their

201

father's house searching for him. Raul suggested that it would be safer if he collected his father and Eladio from their homes and took them to his fishing boat, which he considered the safest place to meet. Pablo remembered thinking that evening, as he said his goodbyes to his father and brothers, that it might be a year but surely no more before they would meet again.

On entering the care home, Pablo had no expectation that his father would recognise him. The brothers were shown into a sitting room where there were over a dozen frail residents viewing the television in silence, apart from a few who were snoring. In the far corner their father was slumped in an armchair and appeared to be asleep. Raul tapped his forearm and he stirred, looking around as if confused.

'Hi, Papa. Do you recognise this man? It's been a long time since you last saw him and he has come a very long way to see how you are,' Eladio said.

In response, their father smiled at Pablo and nodded his head slowly.

'Who is this man, Papa?' Raul asked.

'It's my brother, but I can't remember his name.'

'This is Pablo, your son. Don't you recognise him?' Eladio asked.

'He's my brother. Sorry, what's your name again? I have a terrible memory.'

'Alberto! Do you like it here? A lovely place, don't you think?' Pablo asked.

'It is a lovely place, Alberto. Have you come far?'

'Yes, it's been a long journey, but it has been worth it to see you again. Do you like the people here? Is the food good?'

'Oh yes, I like the food. Not as good as Mum's food but nothing ever could be, eh Alberto?'

'Nothing could be as good as hers. And the people here, do you like them?' Pablo asked.

'Oh yes. I like them. They're all friendly and kind. I'm lucky to be living here.'

'Do you remember the last time we saw each other?' asked Pablo.

Their father did not respond but kept his gaze on Pablo, while smiling. When Raul started to speak, Pablo made a gesture to allow him to continue uninterrupted. The conversation continued much as Pablo was used to having at work and he showed none of the awkwardness that his brothers felt at their father's confusion as to who he was talking to. Pablo prompted the old man to talk of what he remembered of his youth and when his father got stuck, Pablo moved to another topic. After asking him if he had heard from his son Pablo, his father thought for a moment and then responded, 'He's doing well, very happy, and he has children now. Did you know that, Alberto?'

'I had heard, yes. That's good to know.'

'It is. I always liked that boy of mine. Well, I liked every one of them, truth be told, but Pablo... I knew he would be all right.'

'He is. In fact, as good as he has been in a long time,' replied Pablo.

On the drive back after the visit, the brothers stopped at a roadside bar, with views out over the ocean. Contrary to his brothers' disappointment that their father had not recognised Pablo, or indeed them, Pablo felt happier than he had for a long time at seeing his father so content.

'There was recognition there. Maybe not on the same level that we have. When it comes to people with mental-health issues, if they're not disturbed and if they're happy in their world, then that's fine by me. From what we saw today, Papa is happy and that is such a relief for me.'

'Well, I suppose that's one way of looking at it. I just get frustrated at times at the lack of recognition,' replied Raul.

'I would do too if I were seeing him as regularly as you two do. It's ironic, but perhaps if he were to be more aware of what was going on around him, he would probably be much less happy. To get towards the end of life and to be untroubled... that's the best one can hope for.'

'Yes, you're right, Pablo. I must try to keep that in mind,' replied Eladio.

'Thanks again to both of you for all the care you have put in. I will always be indebted to you. Let's have another beer. Eladio, weren't you going to tell me about your work?'

'Yes, to another beer, but I don't want to spoil today by going on about my work,' replied Eladio.

'Let me get the drinks in,' Pablo insisted. As he returned with the beers, Pablo was uncertain whether he should press Eladio further, but he wanted to give him the opportunity to talk about his life, as it felt like all the focus had been on the lives of every other member of the family, except his.

'Eladio, you don't need to tell me how things have been for you if you don't want to, but I am interested.'

'I think you should tell Pablo. It's a story worth hearing,' added Raul.

Eladio started his tale with when he got out of prison, by which time Pablo had fled the country. He couldn't find any work and after a period it became clear that he had been proscribed by every employer in the city. That compounded the darkness which he couldn't throw off, from when he had been tortured and held in prison for almost two months after the coup. By the time he was released from detention, Eladio was sure that there had been infiltration in the labour and trade-union movement, prior to the coup. The interrogators knew so many details about him and other colleagues, which couldn't have been known otherwise. That was not only his view, but that of others. As a consequence, he felt betrayed, but had vowed to remain active in the fight against the dictatorship, albeit in a much more clandestine way. He indicated that Raul had been key to that decision.

Raul then explained that he had become involved in the underground resistance in the months after the coup. He gave no details of what activities he and Eladio had been involved in, but he made it clear that they had been trained in surveillance and had used firearms in operations against local leaders of the dictatorship. Before they had embarked on that fight, they had focused on finding and eliminating those who had infiltrated and betrayed the local branch of the Socialist Party which they had long been members of.

'Those who participated in betrayal are the worst of the worse. I managed to escape the torture and interrogation and had no idea it was going on until a Chilean friend in Bristol told me that he believed exactly the same as you do. I was shocked, which shows my naivety,' replied Pablo.

'Yes, it's difficult for any of us to come to terms with, especially when it's trusted friends who were the informers. Anyhow, back to how hard it has been to earn a living,' Eladio replied.

Every day, from dawn to dusk, was spent in search of work but only in the local area, as he hated the thought of having to leave Puerto Montt. After over a month of trying, he eventually got work in a new seafood-processing plant, which was an expanding industry, but the companies only issued temporary contracts to their workers and the work was often sporadic. Nobody got a permanent contract except the managers and the law did not allow temporary workers to join a trade union. There was no sick pay and no work on the days when no catch came into port. Then there would be forced overtime when a big catch did arrive.

'So, employment with no security and no rights! Surely things will improve now that the dictatorship has been ended?' Pablo said.

'I have no expectation of things getting better for workers like me, just because a new government has been elected. Perhaps the change of government will give us a platform to fight for a better future, especially if trade unions are allowed to organise again. The real power is not with the Government but with the very wealthy, and a lot of them don't even live in the country,' insisted Eladio.

'I wouldn't disagree, although I'm not sure I have the right to comment on matters in this country as I don't live here now,' replied Pablo.

'You've got every right to comment. It's your country. You had to flee for your life because of your beliefs, not because you chose to leave,' replied Eladio.

'Yes, it's still my country of birth, but my life has been lived for so long now in another country. I am bonded to you, my family, and the few remaining friends here, but my children know nothing other than where they have always lived. Let's talk about something more cheerful, like those crazy times when we were growing up.'

They drank several more beers while reminiscing about their youth and their first girlfriends. After a great deal of laughter, they drove back on what was the last night they would have together before Pablo and his family left for Temuco in the morning. That night, Pablo slept well, having made love with Isabel for the first time since they'd arrived in Chile.

It was the last day before Isabel and Pablo were due to leave Temuco for Santiago where they would be meeting up with Carmen and Manuel, before returning to England. There was an awkwardness among the four adults sat around the dining table. Paula had gone quiet during the meal and insisted on doing all the clearing up by herself. She had just returned to the table having spent an extended period on her own in the kitchen and was sitting in silence. Isabel decided that she had to break the pervading gloom.

'This is our last night, but our time here has been unforgettable. Being with you, Paula, has been the highlight. I will cry tomorrow when leaving but feeling sad is not how this visit should be remembered. We will be seeing each other again before too long. So, let's toast to this brighter future we have before us,' stated Isabel as she raised her glass.

'You're making me cry, Isabel,' replied Paula, as her voice wavered.

'Looks like I'm making myself cry. I was thinking that would be for tomorrow, but one can't dictate one's emotions. But Paula, this is not the crying of the last eighteen years. We do know we will see each other probably no later than next year,' continued Isabel as she got up to hug Paula.

'To your wonderful hospitality, Paula and Nico, which we look forward to reciprocating in the not-too-distant future. Failing that, we will be back here again to take advantage of your generosity. You will never be rid of us now,' Pablo said as he raised his glass.

'We will take you up on a trip to England. When that will be though is not certain, but as things unfold here that should become clearer. So yes, let's celebrate the welcome change blowing through our lives. As for uncertainty, that's nothing new so let's not concern ourselves with that,' replied Nico.

'I want to see where you and your family have found happiness and security. What makes me sad is thinking of how our lives have been driven apart by what happened here in Chile. That separation still seems so cruel to me. For what it's worth, I find it hard to see why you would ever come back to this country to live, much as I would love it if you did,' Paula said.

Chapter 21

For the week following her meeting with Javi, Carmen had been in turmoil. There had been several discussions with her brother Pedro on the impact of that meeting and on what she should do with the information Javi had given her. However, when she and her brother had said their farewells yesterday morning, she was still unsure what she would tell Manuel. It was only when she was lying awake during the night that she had made up her mind to tell him everything about her visit to Javi. Although she could see advantages of saying nothing about Roberto Diez, the thought of concealing that information from Manuel, the person she loved more than anyone, was something she could not live with.

The question was how she should try to convince him not to get involved in pursuing the matter further, or at least not having any direct involvement. Just as she reaffirmed her goal of making Manuel see that it would be the best course of action to do nothing other than pass on the information to others who wanted to pursue Diez, she caught sight of him approaching her table with a beaming smile on his face.

'Great to see you, my love. Did everything go well?' Manuel asked as they hugged.

'It's been an interesting time, and it was wonderful to see Pedro in particular. I am so happy to be with you again, but you have to go first and tell me what has been happening with you, and then I'll fill you in on my news.'

Manuel was reluctant to agree but as Carmen insisted, he began to recount all that happened on his trip to Valparaiso and since he'd returned to Santiago a couple of days earlier. He talked of his admiration for his sister, Irena, and of how independent she was, but it was how his father had behaved that had most surprised him. Manuel had been left wondering whether his father had changed so much since he last saw him, or whether he had always misunderstood his father. He acknowledged that his father's mobility was restricted, but he had been surprised about how sharp he still was. His father had even picked up on his intention to pursue Roberto Almagro, although he warned him against doing that. It was his empathy and warmth that Manuel had found so unexpected, and as a consequence, his time in Valparaiso had been much better than he had feared it would be.

He told Carmen of his intention to now write regularly to his father and he hoped they would be able to return to Chile to see him, perhaps next year or the year after, although it was more likely that Irena would come to see them in Bristol before that.

'Your father's advice to you about not taking matters into your own hands – I think that's particularly good advice. I hope you're going to keep your promise to him on that.'

He then recounted his trip to Antofagasta, explaining that after the difficult encounter with Jorge's brother, it had ended well with his meeting his sister, Teresa.

'It was a shock to learn that his brother was an informant but the big issue remains finding Almagro. I met with several old contacts from the party, but nobody has any information on whether he is still alive, let alone what he is doing or where he is living now. Anyhow, how have you fared?' Manuel asked.

'The meetings with friends in Santiago did not go well. We don't have very much in common except memories of the past. Nobody was comfortable talking about what had happened under the dictatorship. On the other hand, my brother Pedro was helpful in explaining how things, or rather how people, had changed in differing ways. If nothing else I feel I have a better understanding of how this country has changed.'

'Yes, I think those of us returning here after a lifetime away have a lot to get our heads round. I'm sorry to hear that about your old friendships. How was it when you got to La Serena? Did you meet up with Javi?'

Carmen nodded her head and proceeded to tell him all that had happened. The colour drained from Manuel's face when she told him of Javi's betrayal. When she moved on to set out all that Javi had said about Roberto Almagro, Manuel's mouth fell open. He suddenly stood up, staring into the distance, before he sat back down.

'I need a drink. Do you want anything?' Manuel asked.

'I'll have a coffee.'

Manuel returned with the coffee and a large brandy for himself.

'Carmen, I'm in shock. What you've told me of Javi is an astounding revelation. I didn't have any idea, although I always felt there was something about him that didn't fit. I just thought that he was a person who was awkward in his relationships with people. It somehow seems so obvious now. How did none of us spot it?'

'I've been asking myself that question especially given that it was me who had a relationship with him. Looking back, I can see things that didn't register with me at the time, and in retrospect, maybe should have. It has left me feeling soiled, like I felt in captivity, but I also feel rage like never before. How dare he even think I would understand, let alone forgive him.'

'Do you think he expected that from you?'

'Why would he have written to me, tell me he was dying and get me to visit him if he wasn't looking for forgiveness?'

'Perhaps. I just can't understand anyone like that. There can't be anything worse than working to get someone's trust – or worse, getting somebody to love you – but only as part of a plan to betray that person.'

'He was convinced that his being so-called *honest* with me now would somehow make it better. How did he ever arrive at that? One thing is for sure, I won't let this bring me down. For me, he does not exist now. In truth, the Javi I thought I knew, never did exist.'

Manuel began to describe how the information about Roberto Diez had impacted on him. Although he had already arrived at the view that he had been an informer, knowing now that he had been in charge of one of the most notorious centres for the torture and killing of so many people filled him with hatred and a thirst for revenge. Manuel admitted that he knew he couldn't kill anyone, not even Roberto Diez, but he did want him tracked down and he wanted to confront him about the deaths of his four friends, which he believed he must have been responsible for.

'Manuel, those people are dangerous. They are not going to let someone track them down and expose them. Besides, they are hardly likely to be without protection, so how do you think you would ever get to him?'

'There are people who would have no trouble killing him were they given the chance. I need to talk to them to see what can be done. There is no avenue to justice through the legal system given that people like Diez have protection from prosecution. What else can I do other than collaborate with those who can deliver another form of justice?'

'Let's not call it *justice*. That can only be delivered by a judicial process where all the facts are established and then judgement and punishment determined by people with no personal interest in the case.'

'I don't think you're right on that. Justice and the process of administering it are not one and the same thing. The fact is there is no judicial process to deal with this and there is no prospect of one being put in place. Doesn't it amount to *injustice* if those who have tortured and killed people go free?'

'You're scaring me, Manuel. Our future life together is being put at serious risk if you embark on this.'

'Carmen, I promise again that I will not be doing any killing, but I need to act on this. If I walk away, I will feel forever complicit in not getting justice for my friends, when I had the opportunity to do so. Our future together is all that is worth living for, but it won't work if I'm plagued with guilt.'

'Okay, but I want us to discuss this with Isabel and Pablo. They are our closest friends. If after that, you still want to go ahead, I will return to England as I can't be of any help to you here. I'll await you there, but I have to say that I have a dreadful feeling about how this will end.'

The following day, Isabel, Pablo and their two children arrived in Santiago to stay with friends for a few days before their return to England. With their friends happy to child mind, they had arranged to meet up with Carmen and Manuel in a bar in the centre of the city, to catch up on what they had each been doing. During the initial greetings, Isabel sensed that Carmen was distracted and not as engaged as she'd expected. She wondered whether this was due to Carmen's meeting with Javi, but decided it was best to wait for Carmen to open up about whatever was troubling her.

Pablo and Isabel were full of noisy excitement and impatient to share their experiences and impressions of their time with family and friends in the south of Chile, but it wasn't long before Isabel became aware that both Carmen and Manuel were contributing very little.

'Is there something wrong?' Isabel asked.

'Yes. I need to tell you about my meeting with Javi. I'm sorry to spoil things but you need to know what happened, or rather what he told me,' replied Carmen.

She set out in detail what she referred to as 'Javi's betrayal,' but at that stage made no mention of what he had told her about Roberto Almagro. Pablo and Isabel sat in silence, drained of all the vigour and passion they had shown earlier. Manuel sat silent and still, showing no emotion, as if he was disinterested. Carmen finished her account with her voice breaking and a single tear rolled down her cheek.

'Oh Carmen, how awful, you having to deal on your own with such a shocking revelation. I can scarcely take it in myself. He's an evil bastard. I never trusted him, but this is beyond belief,' said Isabel as she leaned over to take Carmen's hand.

'I don't know what to say. I had no idea whatsoever. Thinking of him befriended by everyone… It's like there was a serpent among us and we didn't notice,' added Pablo.

'How could any of us have known, Pablo? You could believe this happening in Chile, but not on the other side of the world. The first I knew of the possibility was when the Commission reported that the dictatorship had planted people abroad to track those in exile. Yet I never thought that would extend to us in Bristol, of all places,' responded Manuel.

'I still don't understand why he would want to tell you about something so shameful, Carmen. Did he explain why?' Isabel asked.

'Do you want me to explain what else he said?' Manuel asked.

Carmen nodded.

Manuel set out all that Javi had also told Carmen about Roberto Almagro, whose real name was Roberto Diez. Diez had a leading role in the torture and killing of many of those the dictatorship had hunted down. He had been Javi's boss in that long period of espionage. Although Manuel had already suspected Almagro because of the absence of his name from the lists of those killed or disappeared in the Commission's report, he was shocked by the extent of his murderous role and was now convinced that Diez had been involved in the killing of his friends.

'But why was Javi motivated to tell all this to Carmen? I don't understand,' stated Isabel in exasperation.

Carmen intervened to explain that Javi told her that he had changed his views or perhaps his allegiance – she couldn't remember his precise words. Javi claimed that when Pablo informed him all those years ago about the rapes and the horror she had suffered, he had known nothing about any of it until then. He said that prompted the start of his change of allegiance, because she was the only woman he had ever loved. Things didn't change right away as it was some time after that he left England, but he claimed he had never provided anything other than unimportant information on exiles in Bristol or in other parts of England. When he eventually got back to Chile he said that he had nothing more to do with DINA.

'But why tell you about Roberto Almagro or whatever his real name is?' asked Isabel.

Carmen explained that Javi had said it was due to a combination of his respect for Manuel and his love for her. He knew how much Manuel was plagued by guilt about surviving when his friends had not. Javi had presented his reason for telling her about Almagro and where he now lived as his contribution to the resolution to the blight on Manuel's life, and thereby contributing to the future happiness of Carmen. He had called it his final act to counterbalance all the evil things he had done in his life.

'A drop in the ocean more like. I reckon it's one bastard having a grudge against another, who is even worse. Are you sure he's actually dying, Carmen?' Isabel asked.

'Yes, he is. Not even he could disguise the state of his health. He showed the sure signs of someone soon to die of lung cancer. I don't want to talk further about him. I do want to talk about what Manuel intends to do now about Roberto Diez. Tell us, Manuel.'

Manuel started by pointing out that Diez was immune from prosecution owing to the Amnesty Law which the dictatorship had passed. There was no chance of it being rescinded because of how the constitution allowed the armed forces to block any attempt to permit prosecutions. That being the case, he could not live with himself were he to walk away and do nothing. The killing of his friends was a blight on his life that would only get worse if he did not act on this information.

His plan was to seek the help of others better trained and well placed to find and confront Diez. Manuel's sole aim was to elicit Diez's role in the killing of his friends and if possible give them a proper burial. Manuel swore he wouldn't kill anyone, but he knew that was unlikely to be the case for those whose help he had to enlist. His plan was to be part of the tracking down and the confrontation with Diez to get the answers he needed.

'You need to walk away from this, but that's not because I think Diez and his type don't deserve to have justice served on them. It's because what you are suggesting is highly dangerous and I fear for how this will end,' said Carmen.

There was silence for several moments before Isabel spoke.

'I agree with Carmen. I know that it's hard for you, Manuel, but you're not thinking straight. Don't do it, please.'

'How can you ask me to walk away? I just couldn't live with myself. You all know how I have struggled with this. It will never go away, and I'm convinced it will contaminate everything in the future if I don't act now.'

'You're going ahead regardless of what any of us say, aren't you?' Pablo asked.

'It doesn't make me feel good, but yes, I have to.'

'If that is your decision then please listen to me. How well do you know and trust these people who are going to help you? You've had little or no contact with them until fairly recently, and this is a high-risk venture, so I don't think you should do it with them. I have a better, less risky suggestion,' replied Pablo.

Pablo told them of his brothers and their involvement in underground activities. He explained that his brothers had given him little detail, but they were trained in surveillance and in the use of arms and explosives. Given that Diez was located not too far from Puerto Montt where his brothers lived, then surely it was best to talk to them about how to go about this. There was no risk of infiltration or betrayal with his brothers involved, and he was the person who could introduce Manuel to them.

'But Pablo, we're due to fly back to England in a couple of days' time,' Isabel stated.

'Yes, but we have flexible tickets. We could delay our departure.'

'How long for? The children are due back in school in a couple of weeks' time.'

'It won't take long to go down to Puerto Montt to meet up with them and talk it through, but yes, it will take a while for any plan to be drawn up and implemented. Perhaps you and the children should go back to England with Carmen. Manuel and I will join you after this has been done.'

'So, you're getting involved? And the women and children should stay out of it?' Isabel asked.

'No, I don't mean that at all. The alternative is that I stay out of it and Manuel throws in his lot with people he hardly knows, and who know nothing of that region in the south. I don't think Manuel will survive that. I can't let that happen, Isabel. You know that as well as I do,' replied Pablo.

'I really appreciate your friendship and support, Pablo, but you have your wife and children to think about,' Manuel responded.

'You've made your decision, Manuel, as Pablo appears to have made his. I will make mine. The children and I will go back with you, Carmen. I can see there's no talking you out of this, Manuel, and without Pablo and his brothers, I think you will be in serious danger. If that's how it has to be, let's get on with it,' Isabel stated.

'Manuel, I have two conditions. Firstly, you only pursue this through Pablo and his brothers. Secondly, if his brothers decide they cannot help you then you must abandon any attempt to confront Diez. I'm sure that it will result in his killing by those helping you, given the danger for them if he is left free to do what he usually does,' Carmen stated.

'I will go along with all that, my love, thank you. Thank you all for being who you are.'

The plane soared up into the bright blue sky and headed out towards the coastline of the Pacific Ocean, from where it veered back towards the land in a wide loop, having gained the height necessary to fly over the Andes. The long flight back to England had begun and the mountains towered up on either side, some much higher than the plane. That caused Carmen to feel close to a panic before she remembered to breathe in a slow and steady rhythm. After a brief period, she accepted that the plane was on a safe flight path.

'I'm exhausted by the emotion of these last few weeks. If only we were returning home to a carefree future,' said Carmen.

'Indeed! I have the children to deal with so at least I will have that distraction. I want to see you as often as possible until they return, Carmen. Promise me you will do that.'

'I promise. I had imagined the flight back home would be a time to relax and bathe in lots of warm experiences and memories that would leave our longstanding troubles and doubts resolved. Should we all get through this, will there then be any lasting peace for us?'

Chapter 22

They arrived in Puerto Montt just as the blood-red sun was dipping below the horizon. Pablo's brothers awaited them at the quayside where Raul's boat was moored. The brothers gave each other a warm embrace.

'This is Manuel, my best friend.'

They shook Manuel's hand and then looked around for a few moments before Raul picked up both their bags and led them up the footway onto the boat and down into the cabins below deck.

'I think it's best you stay here rather than book into a hotel or rent accommodation. I've told our neighbours here that you're on holiday and intend to do a lot of fishing. They're all good people. Let me get you a beer and then we can talk,' Raul explained.

'Great! I wanted to do some fishing while here. In the meantime, I'll let Manuel tell you his story and you can tell us if you can help,' replied Pablo.

Manuel started by outlining his political activism prior to the coup and how he had met the person he then knew as Roberto Almagro. He outlined what had happened on the day of the coup and the weeks after in captivity, until he was released at the Bolivian border when he thought he was on a journey to his own execution. Having explained what had happened to his friends and the suspicions that had arisen when Almagro was not listed either as killed or disappeared in the Commission's report, he then set out what his partner Carmen had been told while in La Serena.

'Manuel needs help to track Diez down. He needs to know what happened to his friends and what Diez's involvement was in those killings. I've known Manuel since the beginning of exile and I know how troubled and guilt-ridden he's been about surviving when his friends didn't,' added Pablo.

'So, Manuel, you want us to help you find Diez and kill him?' Eladio asked.

'What I want is to know what happened to my friends and if possible, to locate and recover their bodies for a proper burial. I can't kill anyone, even Diez, as much as I wish I could,' replied Manuel.

'That villa in Santiago you say he was in charge of… that's where several of our people were taken to. They were never seen again. You have to realise that a lot of the bodies of the disappeared are not recoverable as they were dumped in the ocean or in lakes. Are you sure it's worth confronting him just to be told that by the bastard?' Raul asked.

'I need to know one way or the other. If there is a chance to give my friends a proper burial, then I have to pursue that. I also want to know why I was spared and they weren't. That's always bothered me down through the years.'

'Manuel, to be blunt, there is no way of confronting him without someone being killed. It's either him or one or all of us. These people won't put up with a threat of exposure, even though they don't need to worry about being prosecuted. What I'm saying is this can't be done without him being killed. You need to accept that if we're to go any further,' Raul replied.

'If that's how it must be, then so be it. What I am clear about is that I won't be the one to kill him.'

'That's fine with us but you need to accept that you might be implicated by association. We will do everything we can to avoid that, but there are no guarantees about what might happen. Do you accept that, Manuel?' Eladio asked.

'Yes, I do.'

'Okay, here's what we propose to do. We will talk with a small group of our comrades. Given Diez is implicated in the killing of our people at that villa in Santiago, I expect our comrades will want to act regardless of your reasons. Meanwhile, the only talk of this is among us. No mention of this to anybody else. Agreed?' Raul asked.

'Agreed!' replied Manuel and Pablo.

The boat arrived back at port after a night's fishing. The crew began to offload the catch with a speed and determination that Pablo and Manuel admired while they watched from the deck, as instructed by Raul, who had insisted that they would only hinder the operation if they tried to help.

'That will probably be his view of us if they decide to track down Diez. I wouldn't blame him, as we are a pair of amateurs to them,' said Manuel.

'They know what they're doing but my brothers appreciate how important this is to you. They won't exclude you, but they will insist on full control if they take it on. Remember, they're the ones most exposed as they will continue to live around here afterwards,' replied Pablo.

'Yes, I appreciate that, and I accept that they have the experience and know how to do this. If it would be best to delay our departure from Chile afterwards, my sister Irena has told me that she could provide a haven for us in Valparaiso, if we need one. She owns a couple of properties and is very discreet. I trust her with my life. You'll like her.'

'Let's talk about that with Raul and Eladio… if they decide

they are going to proceed. We need to take their advice and instructions on what we do to get back home safely to England. Raul told me this morning that they would tell us of their decision this evening. Are you still keen to go ahead?'

'I don't have any option but to follow this through. I can't have this continuing to hang over me. It has contaminated so much of my life. If your brothers say they won't proceed, then I will accept that as I have promised Carmen, and of course you and Isabel. If that's the case we will leave for home, via Valparaiso to see my father and sister, if that's acceptable to you?'

'Yes, that would be fine for a couple of days, but I would want to get back as soon as I can. In the meantime, let's have breakfast and then get some exercise before meeting my brothers this evening.'

It was dark by the time Raul and Eladio arrived back at the boat. Pablo and Manuel had spent the day walking around the bay trying to distract themselves from what might await them, but in the past two hours they had been sitting in the lower cabin trying to amuse themselves by playing cards, which they could not maintain for more than half an hour.

'We have talked with our people, and we will start surveillance of Diez tomorrow morning. That will continue for two weeks and then we will meet to make a decision on what we do next,' explained Raul.

'I don't understand what that means, Raul. It sounds like no decision has been made,' replied Pablo.

'Yes and no. We have decided to start the operation and that means gathering information on patterns of behaviour, so that we can plan the next stage to best manage the risks before we draw up and then launch a plan of action. We can't eliminate all the risks of course, and you need to accept that.'

'What will our roles be in the surveillance?' Manuel asked.

'You won't have any role in that. It's best that's left to those who have done it many times before and what's more, to those who are familiar with the area. We have enough people who fit those requirements,' replied Eladio.

'Two weeks seems a long time. Are you sure there's nothing for us to do to help?' Manuel asked.

'You need to leave this to us. We're not cutting you out. If and when we get to Diez, you will be there to question him. In the meantime, Eladio and I think it might be best if you both went off somewhere to relax and sightsee and only come back here when we're ready to act. It's best you're not seen around these parts during this period. Can you do that?' asked Raul.

'I hadn't anticipated that so I can't think where to go. Manuel, what do you think? Your sister?' Pablo asked.

'Yes, we could do that. I'll contact her tomorrow morning. She lives in Valparaiso.'

'Great! Pablo, phone me two weeks today at seven o'clock in the evening. If I invite you to come down to our party, that means you come back here to the boat. Don't tell your sister anything about this. It's best that she knows no more than that you are coming back to Puerto Montt to say your goodbyes before leaving for England. Is that clear?' Raul added.

'Yes. One thing I did want to ask is about leaving here afterwards. Do we leave immediately after the operation?' Pablo asked.

'I was going to come onto that. When you get the invite from me, before you leave Valparaiso to come back here, you must book your flight for England for no less than seven days later. They will be checking all departures from the country for a few days after he goes missing. You will be driven to Santiago after the encounter with Diez. What you do in the time before you fly back to England is for you to decide,' replied Raul.

Pablo and Manuel left Puerto Montt the next morning and took a flight back to Santiago and then a coach ride to Valparaiso. They met up with Irena in a café by the seafront. Manuel had explained over the phone that he would like to take her up on that offer of a place to spend time in Valparaiso. She had brought the keys together with directions to the property.

'How long will you be staying for?' asked Irena.

'At least two weeks. We then need to leave again, but would it be okay if we came back to stay for a week before going home to England?' Manuel asked.

'No problem. You keep the keys and when you leave the first time, just let me know when you're coming back. Dad will be happy to see you again, but I haven't told him, as I didn't know if you intended to see him.'

'Yes, tell him I'll call in at the end of the week with a friend I'm on holiday with.'

'Great. It's a pleasure to have you here, and to meet you, Pablo. I'm happy to meet up with you both whenever you want. Phone me. Enjoy your stay.'

'One last thing, Irena. When we leave the first time, I'll let you know the night before. Sorry for the short notice but it needs to be that way. We will phone you when we return.'

'I'm glad that you are making progress, Manuel. I hope that you get the outcome you deserve but be careful.'

The challenge was to prevent time from standing still. Each day began with the realisation that it was not yet the day when they might be told to return to Puerto Montt. Every evening, Manuel prepared a list of activities to be undertaken the following day, so that they could escape that daily realisation, soon after it hit them. In the first few days, it took some time for Pablo to shake off his depression, but by mid-morning he had dragged himself out of it. By the end of the first week, they had settled into a routine, one that ensured that each day differed in some way from what they had done the day before.

In the time since Manuel discovered that Roberto Diez had been an undercover spy, he had gone through countless scenarios of the questions he would ask and the potential responses, should he have the opportunity to be in a room with Diez. He considered that he had exhausted all possibilities so while in Valparaiso, Manuel tried to avoid all thoughts of what awaited on his return to Puerto Montt. Their daily itinerary included a mix of activities such as visits to a variety of restaurants and bars, meetings with Irena, trips to art galleries, exploring different areas of the old city, walks along the bay in each direction, and an hour each evening for reading. After the first visit to see his father, when he went with Pablo, he then visited alone every second day. That arrangement also allowed Pablo some time on his own, which he had asked for.

The trip to the poet Neruda's house at Isla Negra about thirty miles south of the city was held over for the end of the second week so that Manuel had something to look forward to in what he knew would be a period of growing impatience. On the thirteenth day since their arrival in Valparaiso, Manuel made the journey on his own and boarded a mid-morning bus for Isla Negra. His excitement drained away when he arrived only to find the house closed to the public.

It was a stormy day with the ocean tumultuous, launching furious waves which crashed onto the shoreline that the house overlooked. Manuel wandered around the gardens for a few minutes but only felt a sadness that he had not anticipated, remembering that Neruda had stated that he wished to be buried here by the ocean, but that had not been permitted by the dictatorship. There was speculation that the new government was about to allow his family to have him buried in the place of his choosing, but that thought did not lessen his sadness, as it reminded him of his lost friends, and made him wonder if he would ever succeed in getting them laid to rest in a marked grave.

The wind and the driving rain saturated him with doubts and fears of what lay ahead in the next few days. He turned his back on the angry ocean and returned to Valparaiso on what felt like the longest bus ride of his life, hoping the trip was not a bad omen. For the first time, he was questioning the wisdom of what he had embarked on.

The following day, Pablo awoke to a feeling of nervous anticipation that would heighten as the day went on. There was a plan, as with any other day, but both of them could not stop counting down the hours to seven o'clock in the evening when Pablo was due to call Raul. The hour before the call they spent in a bar where there was a public phone box. In order to avoid the phone being in use at the crucial time, Manuel used the phone to make a long call to Irena twenty minutes before the appointed time for the call to Raul, while Pablo stood outside to make sure he was first in line to use the call box after Manuel finished. At seven o'clock, Manuel ended his call to Irena and returned to the bar. Pablo dialled Raul's number while Manuel sat drinking a beer at a table in the corner. After a few minutes Manuel saw Pablo approaching. He took a deep breath.

'We have the invitation. We are to arrive no earlier than five o'clock the day after tomorrow. We'll be picked up from the airport. Let's try and book the flights this evening and should there not be any seats available, we can take a train that will get us there on time.'

'That's such a relief! I was wondering how we would cope if there was to be a further period of waiting. Let's go to the travel agent just along the street and get the arrangements fixed.'

The flights to Puerto Montt were booked for the day after tomorrow, arriving in the early evening. They had several more drinks while they finalised what they would do on their last day. The primary task was to arrange their return flights to England and send telegrams to both Carmen and Isabel informing them of when they would be arriving back on the other side of the world.

'We should take Irena out to dinner tomorrow evening, if she's up for that,' suggested Pablo.

'I'd rather not. I feel too nervous. We'll do that when we return before our flights back to England. I'll phone her and tell her we'll be away for the next few days. Is that okay with you?'

'Of course. It will all turn out fine, Manuel, I promise. I trust my brothers with my life.'

Chapter 23

'Where are we?' I ask.

'It's best you don't know,' replied the driver, who I had never seen before he picked us up at the airport in Puerto Montt.

When he approached us at the Arrivals gate, he didn't give his name and had told us not to address each other or anybody else by their name under any circumstances. He instructed us to adopt the habit immediately, so that we were accustomed to doing so by the time we arrive at our destination.

We've now been driving for over an hour and dusk has descended. Not a word is spoken among us. Without warning, the truck lurches off the road to the right and we're thrown from side to side on the rough track that the truck is being driven too fast on. I remember being thrown backwards and forwards in the back of a van many years before, but I don't feel frightened this time.

I can see nothing but thick tree boughs in the headlights as the truck moves uphill at a cautious pace on a narrow, winding track. From time to time, it almost comes to a halt but doesn't stop when I think it's about to. I know that I'm near my journey's end – a journey I have often doubted I would ever complete.

At that moment I catch sight of them. They are accompanying me – my long-lost friends, tortured and killed but residing in my head ever since. They glide just ahead of the truck, beckoning me to follow. Sara and Julia on one side of the track and Jose and Pepe on the other. Sara stops and looks back at me, smiling.

'Thank you for refusing to forget. We will never forget you,' she calls out to me.

The guilt of almost twenty years drains away. I'm about to reply when all of a sudden the truck veers to the left, and they are gone.

A clearing emerges and we come to a halt by the side of two other trucks, some way from a log cabin that looks too small to be someone's home. There's a dim light coming through a curtain on the window of the cabin. Two men in balaclavas approach our truck, where we sit awaiting instructions on what we should do next. The door of the truck is pulled open, and we jump out to embrace the two men.

'Listen carefully. Diez is being held inside. Two comrades are guarding him. Here's your balaclava. If you're going in, then put it on,' he says to my friend.

'I advise you to put this on. I know you are going to reveal who you are to him, but it's best he does not know what you look like now,' he says to me.

'Okay,' I hear myself say as I pull it over my head.

'You have no more than twenty minutes. You might not need that long as he could refuse to respond. We've told him that he will be released if he cooperates with you and tells you what you want to know. Don't worry though, he won't be talking to anyone else after this.'

I feel nothing at hearing Diez's death sentence. We're offered handguns, but I shake my head. I'm surprised to see my friend take one and check the barrel and lock, showing he is well used to handling a gun, which I had never known about him.

'Our two comrades inside are armed and should Diez try anything, they will deal with him. You shouldn't need to use the gun. Let's go.'

By the back wall of the room, a middle-aged man with thin, greying hair is sitting on a simple wooden stool, leaning forwards and looking at me in an inquisitive manner. He has dried blood above his lips from a nosebleed and a swelling on his left temple. It's the person I knew as Roberto Almagro. At long last! How many times have I rehearsed this?

'I know who and what you really are. Do you remember me?' I ask.

He ignores me and asks for a cigarette. One of the armed men standing guard lights a cigarette and hands it to him as the other aims his gun at Diez.

'Are you too afraid to let me see you?' Diez asks me.

I pull off my balaclava and stare at him.

'We do meet in strange places.'

'There will be no betrayal this time. You had my friends killed and I know you tortured and killed many others.'

'A lot of people were killed back then. I don't remember your friends specifically. What were their names?'

'Jose Sanchez, Sara Garcia, Pepe Lopez, and Julia Ruiz. All listed as disappeared from the villa in Santiago that you were in charge of. No doubt you never even bothered to read the report of the National Commission for Truth and Reconciliation.'

'I did read it. Full of lies and distortions!'

'You need to tell me where the remains of my friends are, if you want to survive this.'

'That's simple. Two of them were dumped far out in the ocean. The other two were disposed of in some wood, a few miles outside the city. There will be records of where they are buried.'

'You're a callous bastard. I want the detailed information.'

'I'm the only person who can provide the information you want.'

'How were they killed? Who were the two dumped in the ocean?'

'I don't know precisely how they were killed, nor do I have the names of the two thrown from the plane, but I can get that information for you.'

'Not good enough. I need more than that. I want names of those who killed them, how they were tortured and killed, the dates and where they were killed and dumped.'

'You don't think I have that information in my head, do you? I know where to get it though. You will never get it as long as I am held here.'

'You're not in any position to bargain. You were in charge for all those years, but not here and not now.'

'And I am not stupid enough to believe that I will be freed if I give you the information you are asking for. How did you find out about me?'

'There you go again. You don't ask the questions, you answer them.'

'Don't you want to hear why you were spared?'

'It doesn't matter to me now.'

'I'll tell you anyway. It was because you were less dangerous than your friends. You were a politician, more an orator than one who acts, and certainly less prone to the reckless commitment that your friends showed. They needed taking out because—'

'So I was spared because I was less of a threat to you and your kind?'

'Yes, but also because you were more useful alive than dead. There was an advantage in letting eloquent people like you go, as you attract the dangerous ones who had escaped and who we needed to keep track of. Yes, there were people like me spying on people like you, even though you were living thousands of miles away.'

'I despise you and your kind.'

'All that we did, we did for our country.'

'Lies and deceit! You set out to cripple the economy, but you saw that the Socialist Government was gaining support despite your efforts at sabotage. So, you and your rich associates decided democracy was not working in your interests. With the support of your American friends, you overthrew the government and embarked on a reign of terror, where everyone opposed to you was hounded and tortured, with thousands killed.'

'We did our duty and ended the chaos.'

'The chaos you worked so hard to create. You dress up your motives and deeds as patriotism when your only allegiance is to keeping power and wealth in the hands of the few. You and your type already have much more than you will ever need, but woe betide anyone who tries to stop you acquiring more or threatens to share some of this country's wealth more widely.'

'You and your type got what you deserved.'

A well of hatred rises up in me. As I gaze at him and see only evil, I know that nothing I say will make any difference. The faces of my dead friends float into my mind and without realising it I'm doing it. My hand reaches out to grab the gun from my friend…

'Let's go. He's not worth it,' my friend says, as he pulls the gun away from my reach. I stare at Diez, loathing everything about him, not least that mocking smile he now has on his face. I turn and start walking towards the door, accompanied by nothing but fury and frustration.

'Evil bastard!' I hear from behind me.

There is the deafening sound of a single gunshot. I turn to see Diez lying on the floor, blood streaming from his head, turning his grey hair red. His body spasms and then lies still. Two men rush in and look from the dead body on the floor to my friend. He takes off his balaclava, hands over the gun to one of them and fixes his eyes on me, while nodding his head. He shows not a trace of shock nor regret at what he has just done.

'Killing him was for me to do and I did it for all those he terrorised… for those he tortured, raped, mentally destroyed, humiliated and killed. And equally, for all their loved ones whose lives have been blighted as a result.'

'You two need to leave now. We'll deal with this. Don't worry, nobody will ever find him at the bottom of the Pacific.'

We are escorted out to the truck. Just as I am about to climb into the back of it there is the sound of a baby crying.

'Where is she? I can't leave my baby behind,' I cry out while running back to the cabin.

Several people catch hold of me. I'm struggling to breathe as they drag me towards the truck… The back door is flung open… They throw me into the truck, headfirst.

My eyes are open. I feel a throbbing pain on the side of my head. My breathing is short and fast. There is light coming through the doorway from the landing and I realise that I'm lying on the floor by the side of our bed. A baby's crying is coming from downstairs. Pulling myself up from the floor, I rush down to the bottom of the stairwell where my wife is trying to console our baby daughter, Sofia, who is crying as if the worst has happened.

'What's going on? There was such a thud. I stopped feeding her to come upstairs to see what had happened,' my wife explains.

'I had a dream, but it wasn't the nightmare. That's gone! In the dream, I heard Sofia crying and was running to get her. I must have fallen out of bed somehow and that woke me up. I'll make you a hot drink.'

By the time I come back from the kitchen, my wife is looking down at Sofia who has finished feeding and is struggling to stay awake in her mother's arms. The baby catches sight of me and breaks into a beaming smile.

'Isn't she adorable? Do you think babies smile with such conviction because they have no past to worry about and no idea of a future?' I ask.

'Perhaps! You smile a lot more these days. Is that because your past is resolved?'

'It doesn't hang over me like it used to.'

'Let's go back to bed and get some sleep. We've got a big day coming up, with the book launch and the party afterwards with all our friends. What about writing another novel?'

'It's unlikely. I'm just happy that the book is written, as I doubted it ever would be. Recently, I've started to write poetry again which I thought was lost to me forever.'

'So, a return to something of your past! When will we go back to Chile?'

'Next year. We'll spend time with our relatives and friends there. Chile has changed and we're no longer who we thought we still were. We will never stop fighting for justice for those horrendous crimes during the dictatorship, but our life is right here, right now, among those who have seen us through the uncertainties and nightmares that haunted our lives for so long.'

Author's Note

On September 11 1973 the Chilean armed forces launched a coup against the democratically elected government of Chile. Within hours the president, Salvador Allende, lay dead and a military junta presided over by General Augusto Pinochet took power. There followed an intense political repression which resulted in political killings and 'disappearances,' the imprisonment or exile of countless Chileans, and the widespread use of torture.

Both in Chile and abroad, political killings, disappearances, and torture came to be considered as the worst abuses of the military regime. It committed many other human rights violations, including massive arbitrary imprisonment and exile, as well as attacks on other civil liberties. The method of disappearances was systematically applied during the first four years of military rule. Victims were kept in clandestine detention, subjected to torture and eventually summarily executed. Their bodies were disposed of in secret. It is estimated that 3,200 civilians were killed or disappeared and up to 40,000 tortured. Many more fled the country.

In 1978, an amnesty law was decreed by the military government. The effect of it was that, with the exception of one crime (the bomb assassination ordered by DINA of Orlando Letelier in Washington, D.C., in September of 1976) all human rights violations committed prior to the date of that decree would remain in impunity.

Soon after the coup, a coalition of churches led by the Catholic Church established the Committee for Peace, which as of 1976 became the Vicariate of Solidarity of the Catholic Archdiocese of Santiago. The Vicariate helped thousands of victims of the political repression and their families. It documented every case which came to its attention and was a crucial source of information on human rights abuse in Chile.

In March 1990, after seventeen years of human rights abuses including the suppression of political parties and trade unions, the dictatorship ended. The new democratic government set up the National Commission for Truth and Reconciliation to investigate, but only those human rights abuses that had resulted in death or disappearance. It took many years before only a few of the perpetrators of these killings were prosecuted. Few perpetrators of the many more crimes of torture and other human rights abuses were ever charged. During the dictatorship, the Mapuche people lost most of their land. The dictatorship also applied a strict monetarist economic policy, which greatly increased poverty and inequality.